THE

LED-HORSE CLAIM

UNDERGROUND.

THE

LED-HORSE CLAIM

A Romance of a Mining Camp

BY

MARY HALLOCK FOOTE

AUTHOR OF "FRIEND BARTON'S CONCERN," "A STORY OF
THE DRY SEASON," ETC.

ILLUSTRATED BY THE AUTHOR

THE GREGG PRESS / RIDGEWOOD, N. J.

First published in 1882 by James R. Osgood & Co.
Republished in 1968 by
The Gregg Press Incorporated
171 East Ridgewood Avenue
Ridgewood, New Jersey, U.S.A.

Copyright© 1968 by
The Gregg Press, Inc.

Library of Congress Catalog Card Number: 68-20012

Printed in the United States of America

AMERICANS IN FICTION

In the domain of literature the play may once have been the chief abstract and chronicle of the times, but during the nineteenth and twentieth centuries the novel has usurped the chief place in holding the mirror up to the homely face of society. On this account, if for no other, the Gregg Press series of reprints of American fiction merits the attention of all students of Americana and of librarians interested in building up adequate collections dealing with the social and literary history of the United States. Most of the three score and ten novels or volumes of short stories included in the series enjoyed considerable fame in their day but have been so long out of print as to be virtually unobtainable in the original editions.

Included in the list are works by writers not presently fashionable in critical circles—but nevertheless well known to literary historians—among them Joel Chandler Harris, Harriet Beecher Stowe, Thomas Bailey Aldrich, and William Gilmore Simms. A substantial element in the list consists of authors who are known especially for their graphic portrayal of a particular American setting, such as Gertrude Atherton (California), Arlo Bates (Boston), Alice Brown (New England), Edward Eggleston (Indiana), Mary Wilkins Freeman (New England), Henry B. Fuller (Chicago), Richard M. Johnston (Georgia), James Lane Allen (Kentucky), Mary N. Murfree (Tennessee), and Thomas Nelson Page (Virginia). There is even a novel by Frederic Remington, one of the most popular painters of the Western cowboy and Indian—and another, and impressive minor classic on the early mining region of Colorado, from the pen of Mary Hallock Foote. The professional student of American literature will rejoice in the opportunity afforded by the collection to extend his reading of fiction belonging to what is called the "local-color movement"—a major current in the development of the national belles-lettres.

Among the titles in the series are also a number of famous historical novels. Silas Weir Mitchell's *Hugh Wynne* is one of the very best fictional treatments of the American Revolution. John Esten Cooke is the foremost Southern writer of his day who dealt with the Civil War. The two books by Thomas Dixon are among the most famous novels on the Reconstruction Era, with sensational disclosures of the original Ku Klux Klan in action. They supplied the grist for the first great movie "spectacular"—*The Birth of a Nation* (1915).

Paul Leicester Ford's *The Honorable Peter Stirling* is justly ranked among the top American novels which portray American politics in action—a subject illuminated by other novelists in the Gregg list—A. H. Lewis, Frances H. Burnett, and Alice Brown, for example. Economic problems are forcefully put before the reader in works by Aldrich, Mrs. Freeman, and John Hay, whose novels illustrate the ominous concern over the early battles between labor and capital. From the sweatshops of Eastern cities in which newly arrived immigrants toiled for pittances, to the Western mining camps where the laborers packed revolvers, the working class of the times enters into various other stories in the Gregg list. The capitalist class, also, comes in for attention, with an account of a struggle for the ownership of a railroad in Samuel Merwin's *The Short-Line War* and with the devastating documentation of the foibles of the newly rich and their wives in the narratives of David Graham Phillips. It was Phillips whose annoying talent for the exposure of abuses led Theodore Roosevelt to put the term "muck-raker" into currency.

While it is apparent that local-color stories, the historical novel, and the economic novel have all been borne in mind in choosing the titles for this important series of reprints, it is evident that careful consideration has also been given to treatments of various minority elements in the American population. The Negro, especially, but also the Indian, the half-breed, Creoles, Cajuns—and even the West Coast Japanese—appear as characters in various of these novels or volumes of short stories and sketches. Joel Chandler Harris's *Free Joe* will open the eyes of readers who know that author solely as the creator of humorous old Uncle Remus. And there is a revelatory volume of dialect tales, written by a Negro author, *The Conjure Woman* by Charles W. Chesnutt.

In literary conventions and the dominating attitudes toward life, the works in the Gregg series range from the adventurous romance illustrated so well by Mayne Reid or the polite urbanity of Owen Wister to the mordant irony of Kate Chopin and the grimmer realism of Joseph Kirkland's own experiences on bloody Civil War battle-fields or the depressing display of New York farm life by Harold Frederic. In short, the series admirably illustrates the general qualities of the fiction produced in the United States during the era covered, just as it generously mirrors the geographical regions, the people, and the problems of the times.

PROFESSOR CLARENCE GOHDES
Duke University
Durham, North Carolina

December, 1967

MARY HALLOCK FOOTE

Mary Hallock Foote was born in Milton, N. Y. in 1847, and died in 1938. She studied art in New York City, and after her marriage in 1876 to Arthur de Wint Foote, a civil and mining engineer, she lived in California, Idaho, and Colorado, places which furnished her with themes and settings for her novels and also for her drawings, six of which appear in *The Led-Horse Claim*.

The Led-Horse Claim is a love story which takes place against the somber, stern, and depressing background of the Colorado gold-fields, where "The restless elements of the Eastern cities; the disappointed, the reckless, the men with failures to wipe out, with losses to retrieve or to forget, the men of whom one knows not what to expect," came to seek their fortunes.

Mrs. Foote describes with cool, keen, and ironic detachment the lives and loves of these misfits. *The Led-Horse Claim* is not a "feminine" book, though it occasionally touches upon the emotional and marital troubles of the mining-camp women. The prose style is "masculine" — clean and concise, and there is neither sentimentality nor rhetoric. There is violence and suffering, but Mrs. Foote, a skilled literary craftsman, avoids playing up mayhem for its own sake, a weakness which appears too often in Jack London's stories. Like London, Mrs. Foote knew her subject matter at first-hand, and saw life as a Darwinian struggle for survival, in which the stupid, the unfortunate, and the kind-hearted generally went under.

The Led-Horse Claim is a remarkable document of frontier life, as well as a work which can stand on its own as imaginative literature. It is a minor classic about an area of America which is surprisingly deficient in regional literature.

PRINCIPAL WORKS: *The Led-Horse Claim* (1883); *John Bodewin's Testimony* (1886); *The Last Assembly Ball* (1889); *In Exile and Other Stories* (1894); *The Chosen Valley; Coeur d' Alene* (1894); *The Cup of Trembling and Other Stories* (1895); *The Little Fig Tree Stories* (1900); *The Prodigal* (1900); *The Desert and the Sown* (1902); *A Touch of Sun and Other Stories* (1903); *The Royal Americans* (1910); *Picked Company* (1912); *The Valley Road* (1915); *The Ground Swell* (1919). Mrs. Foote also illustrated Longfellow's "Skeleton in Armor" and "The Hanging of the Crane."

F. C. S.

CONTENTS.

LIST OF ILLUSTRATIONS.

THE LED-HORSE CLAIM.

I.

THE NEW MINING-CAMP.

THE ark of the mining interests, which had drifted about unsteadily after the break in bonanza stocks in the summer of 1877, had rested, a year or two later, in a lofty valley of Colorado, not far from the summit of that great " divide " which parts the waters of the Continent. It rested doubtfully, awaiting the olive-leaf of Eastern capital. Through the agency of those uncertain doves of promise, the promoter of mining schemes and the investor in the same, the olive-leaf was found, and, before the snows had blocked the mountain-passes, the gay, storm-beleaguered camp, in the words of its exhibitory press, began to " boom."

The snows of that bleak altitude give their first warning while the September sun is still strong; by November they may be said to prevail ; but no disheartening combination of bad weather, worse roads, and worst accommodations at the journey's end, could deter .the pioneers from bearing a city into the unfriendliest spot where such exotic growth ever flourished. Their movement had the absolute conviction, the devotedness, of a crusade. They pressed onward, across the Great South Park, following its white wagon-trails which rise and sink with the long swells of that archæan sea ; pausing in the dreary valley at the foot of the pass, which shelters the caravansary-like town of Fairplay ; struggling upward, in the cold light of early morning, along the mountain sides ; resting again at the last stage-station above the timber-line, where the tough fir forests bend, and fail, and finally give up altogether the ascent of those bare slopes, ever whitening, to the pitiless region of lasting snow ; on again into the strenuous air of the summits, following the pass as it staggers through the wild cañons ; dizzily winding, by weary grades, down to the desolate land of promise.

Foremost in the strange procession were

seen those wandering Ishmaelite families whose
sun-darkened faces peer from the curtains of
their tents on wheels, along every road which
projects the frontier farther into the wilderness.

The discontent and the despair of older
mining-camps in their decadence hastened to
mingle their bitterness in the baptismal cup
of the new one. It exhibited in its earliest
youth every symptom of humanity in its de-
cline. The restless elements of the Eastern
cities; the disappointed, the reckless, the men
with failures to wipe out, with losses to retrieve or to forget, the men of whom one
knows not what to expect, were there; but
as its practical needs increased and multi-
plied, and its ability to pay for what it required became manifest, the new settlement
began to attract a safer population.

Even the hopes of the gold-seeker must be
fed and clothed at an altitude which acts like
the law of natural selection on those who as-
pire to breathe its thin air, sparing only the
sound of heart and lung, and fanning the
nerve-fires into breathless, wasteful energy.
The producer answered the call of the con-

sumer.   Men of all trades followed the miner.
The professions followed the trades, and were
represented, generally, by men in their youth.

It was, perhaps, this immense, though un-
disciplined, force of sanguine youth which
saved the city.   The dangerous elements of
the camp — the mud, the weeds, and the drift-
wood which would have choked a more
sluggish current — were floated and swept
onward by its strong tide.   The new board
sidewalks resounded to the clean step of
many an indomitable, bright-faced boy, cadet
of some good Eastern family, and neophyte
in the business of earning a living, with a
joyous belief in his own abilities and a clean
record to imperil in proving them.   The older
men, who had come with a slightly shaken
faith in themselves, looked half compassion-
ately, half enviously, at these knights of the
virgin shield.

It is said that the first woman of the camp
crossed the range on foot with her husband, a
German miner, and helped him set up the
" poor Lar " of their pine-board shanty during the early snows of the first autumn.   But
those accumulated snows were wasting under

the May sun, and the pass, where they still lay deep, could be traced from a long way off, — a line of white crossing the purple summit of the range, — before the steady migration of wives and children began.

It was a grim sort of nest-building that went on, with discordant chorus of hammer and saw, through the spring and summer and late into the fall of the second year ; but, whatever its subsequent troubles may have been, there was a great show of domestic felicity in the camp at this period. Every incoming stage renewed the bridals of some long-separated couple. Each man who could not send for his own wife, sympathized, with boyish gayety, in the regeneration of his more fortunate comrade. The shop-windows moderated their display of velvet riding-habits, embroidered silk stockings, and pink silk *peignoirs* trimmed with cascades of imitation lace, — their temptations to feminine purchasers taking the more domestic form of babies' knitted hoods and sacques, crash towelling, and the newest patterns in cretonne. Every house over which a woman presided practised a hospitality out of all proportion, in its scope, to the capacities of the rude tabernacle. Every young wife, in her access of happiness, felt a supreme pity for the great army of the unmarried that nightly walked the turbulent streets, between flashes of light from Terpsichorean retreats, and cold glimpses out of the raw city through the open spaces of unbuilt blocks, toward the snow-lit peaks. Many an unshaven bachelor would have smiled with cheerful scorn at·this missionary spirit in his neighbor's wife; a few would have misunderstood it; many profited by it; and many, especially the very young men, went their way, too watchfully absorbed in the keen-edged life of the place to be conscious of any spiritual or social need.

Each night, as the constellations mounted guard above the pass, a redder galaxy lit the dark encampment of hills, where lonely camp-fires, outposts of the settlement, far up on the wooded slopes, signalled the lights from the active mines, or the flaring beacons of smelting-furnaces in the gulch. Two of these distant human lights, shining on the opposite slopes of a fir-lined cañon, which divided them like a river of darkness, had a neighborly look of sympathy in their isolation. The fir-darkened cañon was called Led-Horse Gulch. The lights which beckoned to each other across it shone from the shaft-houses of the Led-Horse and Shoshone mines, between which, it was said, there was open suspicion on the one side and bad faith on the other.

II.

THE TURNING OF A WINDLASS.

ONE August morning of the cool, autumnal summer, a lady, younger than the youngest of the youthful wives of the camp, whose pure, unsunned complexion proved her but lately arrived, rode down into Led-Horse Gulch from the Shoshone side, and, following the trail upward among the aspens, drew rein at the mouth of a small shaft where two men were working a windlass.

She wore no habit; the plaited skirt of her cloth walking-dress permitted her stirrup-foot to show, and a wide-brimmed straw hat shaded the heightened bloom in her cheek. There was an unpremeditation in her dress, and in the vagrant gait of her pony, which might have accounted for this aimless halt at the top of the shaft.

She watched, with idle interest, the taut, wavering rope, as it coiled on the windlass.

The men were hoisting a loaded bucket. She
appeared indifferent to their respectfully curious glances ; they were classified in her mind
as part of the novel human machinery of the
place. She had a dimly appreciative eye for
the fine curves of their powerful backs, as
they leaned and recovered with the circling
cranks that creaked with their weight ;. other-
wise they were not present to her consciousness. From her saddle she could not look
far down into the dark hole and see the
bucket, just visible one moment, then enlarging rapidly with the shortening rope ; nor
could she perceive that it was loaded, not with
precious ores, but with a bulk of that common
human clay of which we are all but metamor-
phic variations. She was, in fact, less interested in the thing coming up than in the
curiously fatalistic manner of its coming. The
wavering rope described a shorter and shorter
circle ; its vibrations ended with a sharp shudder ; a few more, slower turns of the crank,
and the man had arrived at the surface.

Swinging himself, with a practised motion,
from the bucket to a seat on the collar of the
shaft, he looked across at the young girl with

2

undisguised admiration. The look recalled
her at once from the vague, impersonal mood
of her ride.

The men at the cranks let the bucket down
with a run, straightened their backs, and
wiped their damp foreheads and necks.

The unembarrassed youth who rose to his
feet, taking off his hat with a bright, interroga-
tive smile, was also a part of the human machinery of the place, but his part in relation
to the miners at the cranks was that of the
throttle-valve rather than the driving-wheels.

The girl acknowledged his salute by a hot
blush and the slightest of bows, as she turned
her horse's head sharply away from the shaft.
Her position in the face of this new element
had become untenable, and she abandoned it
frankly, making no attempt to explain the
unexplainable. It was not her custom (so she
indignantly apostrophized her girl's wounded
dignity) to be riding about the camp alone,
and waiting at prospect-holes for handsome
young men to be hoisted out of them! It was
an incongruous accident of that incongruous
place!

She had, even with her small knowledge of

young men, perceived this one's quality in his face and manner; but she suffered from the youthful conviction that her own personality must remain inevitably at the mercy of the moment's accidental disguise.

Guiding her horse confusedly over the broken ground, she was startled by a peremptory shout from behind her.

"Look out there, Abrams! The old shaft!"

A miner coming up the hill, warned by the shout, promptly caught her horse's bridle, and forced him back from a sunken space of fresh earth and stones.

The young man who had given the timely order was now at her side. He picked up her whip. The hat he lifted as he offered it was a very bad one, but the head it did its best to disfigure might have been modelled for the head of a young Jason at the time his personal appearance did him such good service at the court of King Æetes.

"In another second you would have been thrown. This is an old prospect-hole filled with loose earth. Your horse would have sunk in it to his knees," he protested, in answer to her look of vexed surprise.

"I wonder my brother permits such a trap to be uncovered," the girl said, with the emphasis of one who finds unexpected relief in another's responsibility for an awkward situation.

"I have not the pleasure of knowing your brother — but the Led-Horse, I believe, has only one superintendent," — he took off his hat again with a gayly ironical bow — "who is at your service, if you will please to command him."

"Am I not on Shoshone ground?" The question was half an assertion.

"I think not. The location stakes follow the gulch, a little on this side of it. You are now about one hundred and fifty feet within the Led-Horse lines."

The young girl could not help smiling at her own discomfiture, when it had reached this point. She hoped the superintendent of the Led-Horse would pardon her for trespassing, and for criticising his management.

The superintendent of the Led-Horse gallantly replied that he could not allow her to call her visit a trespass, and if she liked to ride over his prospect-holes, he would have them all boarded over in that hope.

She made no reply to this somewhat derisive suggestion, and her host of the Led-Horse kept the silence penitently, as he walked at her side through the flickering aspens.

When they had crossed the gulch, he assured her that she was now unmistakably on Shoshone ground, and they parted, with a slightly exaggerated gravity on both sides.

He watched her climbing the hill among the pine trunks that rose rigidly above the fringe of " quaking aspens." Her light figure bent and swayed with her horse's strong upward strides. On the hill-top it was outlined a moment against the fervent blue of the midday sky, and then sank out of sight on the other side.

The young superintendent now turned his attention, with a reflected interest, on himself. He looked himself over, in his close-buttoned pea-jacket, and leggings, buckled to his knees, with the cheerful unconcern of a man who is well aware that no tailor's measurements can altogether frustrate those of nature, at her best.

Had Hilgard been born ten or fifteen years sooner, he might have won more honor in

the camps and fields of the civil war, than
he was likely to gain in frontier mining-
camps. He would have been the idol of his
men, the life of his mess, — a leader of forlorn hopes and desperate charges. His rich-
blooded beauty would have wrung the hearts
of susceptible maidens, marking him in the
ranks of those about to die, when the regi-
ments for the front marched by in farewell
pomp. Like the plume of Navarre, it would
have blazed in the thickest of the fight, and
would have been quenched, perhaps, on one
of those reefs of the dead, which showed,
after the battle, where the wildest shocks of
assault had met the sternest resistance. It
would have marked him a victim without
blemish, fit for the sacrifice.

But in the less heroic time in which his lot
was cast, and in a crude community of trans-
planted lives, adjusting themselves to new
conditions, Hilgard's excess of good looks
was a positive inconvenience. The camp, at
that period of its existence, took more thought
for its roots than its blossoms. Hilgard's
splendid efflorescence was looked upon with
a certain suspicion by the sturdy, masculine

growths around him. Ugly men who relied
upon their fruits, and felt that nature had
disguised them, were not likely to enjoy it.
Men with a small personal vanity of their
own resented it, as a form of insolence, in
their fellow-man. It attracted all the bale-
ful types of womanhood, while many of the
feminine bulwarks of respectability in the
camp regarded it askance as an apotheosis
of the physical life. Not a few of these ladies,
especially those whose own personal attrac-
tions were not conspicuous, honestly doubted
if the virtues of faithfulness and self-denial
could be found in conjunction with a lively
eye-beam, a short upper lip, a head easily
erect above a pair of powerful shoulders, and
an exuberance of color and movement expressive of much unused vitality. Whatever
general foundation there may be for such a
prejudice, the picturesque theories current in
the camp reconciling it, in Hilgard's case,
with his isolated life and obvious indifference
to the social allurements around him, were
far from the prosaic truth.

Hilgard's life was as simple and severe in
its routine as if nature had clothed his soul

in sackcloth instead of purple. It had one
immediate object, — the prosperity of the
Led-Horse, — to which he considered himself
pledged. There was another object, more
remote, but more vital and permanent: the
education of his two half-brothers, — young
lads left to his sole care by the death of both
father and mother. Hilgard's own education
had been at the mercy of the sad breaks in
the lives of those who had watched over it.
He was often lonely, as the captain of a bark
on a long cruise is lonely in mid-ocean, — but
he was in no doubt about his course. He
was not restless from uncertainty of purpose.
He had a fine, youthful scorn of sudden love,
or any sentiment bordering on it. It was his
lonely life, perhaps, which gave such promi-
nence in his thoughts to the small incident of
the morning. He would hardly have admitted
that it was anything in the girl herself. Yet
her face and her slender figure, undulating
upward to the sunny hill-top, were still
vividly before his eyes. He had the keen
instinct about women which men lose when
they care for them too much. All his latent reverence and ideality had responded to

the look in her eyes as they had rested a moment on his. She had blushed, but with a proud, shy girl's disgust at a false position; not helplessly, like a fool, he said to himself. Then he grew hot, thinking of his own careless manner to her, which so ill expressed his sense of her difference from the ordinary pretty girl. If he ever saw her again — of course he would see her again! She was his neighbor, the fair Shoshone — Conrath's sister, whose arrival from the East he had heard of in the camp. Surely she had "snatched a grace" beyond the rules of kinship!

A fragment of a Scotch song, long silent in his memory, woke suddenly, like the first bluebird's note in spring. All the songs and scraps of poetry in which his vagrant moods had been wont to find expression, had been locked in the frosty constriction of his new and perplexing responsibilities: —

"O lassie ayont the hill,
Come ower the tap o' the hill!
Come ower the tap, wi' the breeze o' the hill," —

he hummed to himself, as he strode through the aspens that shivered in the sunshine.

The smooth-stemmed aspens themselves were not more daintily, slenderly rounded, or more unobstrusive in their clear, cool colors. Hilgard did not like showy girls. He held, with most young men, very positive opinions as to the kind of girl he liked, when in reality it was quality, not kind, that interested him.

"Con, my boy!" he recklessly apostrophized his troublesome neighbor, "you 've got my ore in your ore-bins, but if it came to a settlement for damages, there is metal of yours that is more attractive!"

The next instant he rebuked himself for his profanity. His spirits were rising into rebellious gayety, animated by the dramatic implacability of the circumstances that hedged in his lovely foewoman. He laughed aloud, thinking of the innocent audacity with which she had crossed the contested line, and waited for him at the top of his own shaft.

But the mood did not long abide with him. The first bluebird's note is an uncertain harbinger of spring.

As he climbed the trail to his own side of the gulch and looked across to the Shoshone's shaft-houses, its new ore-sheds, the procession of ore-teams loading at the dumps, and all its encroaching activities in full play, and then reviewed his own empty bins and barren underground pastures, the color of romance died out of the prospect.

He walked back to his office, and took up a package of letters from his desk. The one from the president of his company he opened first. It was an order to shut down!

III.

THE SITUATION.

THE Led-Horse had a somewhat dubious reputation in mining circles. The generally unsatisfactory condition of its affairs might have been described in the words of a clever man's impromptu abstract of life, — "Too poor to pay, too rich to quit."

It had opened brilliantly, on a promising vein which had been "stoped out" to a considerable depth, and then had become suddenly barren. The ore-bearing rock was there, precisely similar in character to that which had yielded two hundred ounces of silver to the ton, but the silver was not there.

The expenses of the mine rapidly turned its balance the wrong way. There were calls from the home office for retrenchment, and appeals for money from the mine. Its condition was that of a young man who has spent a small patrimony without having fitted himself for earning his own living. It was altogether probable that the capacity for earning a living was there, but it had become necessary that no time should be lost in developing it.

There was a change in the management, even as the young man, in his altered circumstances, turns from the counsellors of his days of extravagance, to others, better acquainted with hard work and economy. At this juncture, Hilgard had been sent out with a few thousands to expend in enabling the Led-Horse to support himself, and, if possible, to lay up money in dividends; but the dividends were, as yet, a long way in the future.

Hilgard had had four years' practical experience in mines, but this was his first essay in management. He was well aware that he was making it under great disadvantages. He could not put ore into a barren vein, and a prolonged period of unproductive expenditure in prospecting for ore would, in the event of not finding any, count heavily against him in his opening career. It was inevitable that the manager of a mine should be con-

sidered successful according to his fulfilment
of the hopes of the owners; especially when
the owners were half the width of the continent away, and generally ignorant of the
conditions which affect success in the management of mines.

The Shoshone had been in barren rock for
many months. It had small capital and less
credit, when, a short time after Hilgard's
management began, a sudden change took
place in the aspect of its affairs. At the
change of shifts, a daily increasing number of
men were seen around its shaft-houses; new
ore-sheds were put up; its long unused wagon-
roads became deeply rutted by the heavy ore-
teams going and returning from the smelters,
and a rumor pervaded the camp that the lucky
Shoshones had "struck it away up in the
hundreds," and were shipping ore at the rate
of fifty tons a day.

Soon after the Shoshone's prosperity became evident, West, the mining-captain of the
Led-Horse, communicated to his chief his
suspicion that the Shoshone strike had been
made on Led-Horse ground. From the lower
drifts, the sounds which came, through the

intervening rock, from the new Shoshone workings, indicated, to an experienced ear, that they had crossed the boundary line between the claims.

Hilgard had proposed to Conrath, the superintendent of the Shoshone, that a survey should be made through the Shoshone drifts, but at the expense of the Led-Horse, to prove that the boundary line was intact. He put the whole matter lightly, as a possible mistake which either party might have made. Conrath took it by no means lightly. He even appeared to seize upon it as an occasion for giving expression to a latent feeling of antagonism toward Hilgard, which the latter had not been entirely unconscious of. Conrath refused to admit the possibility of his having crossed the line, or to permit any one to explore the Shoshone workings for any purpose whatever. This unexpected irritability on the subject could but increase Hilgard's suspicions. The sounds through the rock, which had been at first very faint, having become, day by day, more distinct, Hilgard had started his defensive drift in the direction of these sounds.

The Led-Horse had not as yet achieved its independence of Eastern capital. The few thousands which had been subscribed at the beginning of Hilgard's management had been spent in " prospecting," with no result as yet, except a little low-grade ore and "favorable indications." The small working force of the mine had been concentrated upon the defensive drift, which was in barren rock.

At this juncture, while the mine was dependent on its monthly drafts from the East, the last of these drafts came back dishonored.

It was a time of bitter excitement to Hilgard. Already the unfortunate Led-Horse, with its hopes and its reverses, had become to him almost like some living thing in his care. It was more than a feeling of pride in his work — it was a passionate personification of it, — more especially since he had been beset by treachery without, as well as by poverty within. Hilgard was experiencing the well-known effect of isolation and responsibility upon a concentrated nature cut off from those varied outlets for its energy which the life of cities and large communities affords. He wrote long, passionate letters on the situation to the home office, where they awoke trouble and perplexity in the mind of the anxious president, but failed materially to alter the situation.

It was during the sultry weather of early September when these vehement appeals from the desperate executive in the West poured in on the worried administration in the East.

The Led-Horse proudly boasted in its prospectuses that its stock was " non-assessable." The men who held it were engaged in larger schemes, which made the fate of the Led-Horse of comparatively little consequence. They were scattered far and wide; on board yachts, at remote fishing and hunting grounds, at watering-places, at home and abroad. To hold a timely meeting of stockholders under these circumstances would have puzzled the most active administration.

It was undeniable that, beyond the office which bore its name, the crisis in the affairs of the Led-Horse made not even a ripple on the " street."

" A draft for two thousand, promptly, will save us ! " Hilgard wrote. " Another week will drive the drift through to the Shoshone

workings, then we can put up a barricade —
shut down — and go into court with a clear
case."

The president trusted, in his reply, that
the " barricade " would be unnecessary. He
deprecated any manifestation in the direction
of expected or intended violence. The law
alone could decide these points, and with this
ultimate decision in view he advised that an
injunction be got out against the suspected
parties, and evidence collected to support it,
while he, in the East, would do his best to
provide money for conducting the subsequent
suit for damages. For the payment of the
running expenses, Hilgard must absolutely
rely on his own resources, or else shut down.
The president concluded by adjuring him to
satisfy himself that his suspicion was correct
before taking any steps in regard to an injunction.

Hilgard leaned back in his chair. He was
mentally replying to the letter he held in his
hand.

" The ' resources ' I am to depend on are in
the hands of the Shoshones, — the proof of
my ' suspicion ' is there, — the evidence for

the injunction is there, — the question is how am *I* to get there ! " He pushed his chair back impatiently. " Can't they understand that it's impossible to shut down with a gang of men unpaid ! "

It had taken a week for his first protest against the order to reach the office ; two weeks for repeated letters to make, so it seemed, any impression on that far-off East to which he looked for succor. After three weeks of waiting the reply had come, and it had brought him only into closer contact with a growing dread, — a dread of the final resort to those wild counsels of primitive justice, from which he felt the strong recoil which marks the passage from irresponsible boyhood to manhood.

The first overt act was before him which would bring him into sharp personal contact with Conrath. The act was now become inevitable, and whether the truth of his suspicion were proved by it or not, the hostility on Conrath's part would follow with certainty.

He went out into the cool starlight and walked about on the bare space of trodden earth outside his office-door.

At sunset the restless winds, whirling in a dervish-like dance along the highways of the camp, scattering straws and chips and scraps of paper, and sinking as suddenly as they rose, in abject heaps of dust by the roadside, had fainted and died away, as if their souls had departed in the soft breeze that wandered, soughing, up the gulch.

Sounds of music floated up from the camp, where it sparkled like a restless reflection of the night sky in the dark valley below. The lights in the two shaft-houses burned warily, eye to eye, across the gulch.

"O lassie ayont the hill!"—the words which had fitfully recurred in his mind through its late preoccupations, came back now with a wistful note. The sweet lassie had kept on her own side of the hill, and he had never gone over to find her. He had never seen her since she had vanished below the sun-illumined hill-top.

Where was she to-night?—dancing at the ball of the "Younger Sons," perhaps, to that music which came faintly to his ear,—or alone, in the hostile Shoshone camp? Conrath had gone over the range two days ago. He liked better to think of her alone, though it could be no part of his to comfort her. Somehow he did not find the dramatic nature of the situation as exhilarating as it had seemed on the day of her innocent invasion.

He went down the hill to a little cabin built against its steepest side, where West sat by his fire, moodily smoking and communing with himself, after the manner of lonely men.

He was a slenderly built, wiry man, of about thirty, with a nervous mouth and a quiet blue eye, which could kindle quickly, as it did now at the sound of Hilgard's step and his bright, authoritative voice. He got up and gave his only chair to his young chief, drawing forward an empty powder-keg and seating himself on its inverted bottom. Hilgard lit a cigarette and sat down astride of the chair with his arms across the back. Both men glowered at the fire in silence.

"A letter came from the 'Old Man' to-day," Hilgard presently said. "It's no use, West. The thing is narrowing down to just this, — we've got to get into the Shoshone workings."

West looked up quickly.

"If Conrath won't go over the ground with us, we must go over it alone, and take the risk of his catching us in there."

West smoked hard for a minute.

"I could have got in there long ago, sir, if you'd said the word."

"I didn't want to say the word! It's an ugly thing to do, — creeping about another man's mine to find out if he's a thief and a liar!"

"Gash can lie; he's an old hand at this game. He made his boast in Deadwood that he could always find plenty of ore as long as his neighbors had any. It's like as not he's fooled Conrath all through. When he struck that streak of ore he couldn't keep from followin' it, any more'n you kin keep a hound off a bear-track. When shall I get in there, sir?"

"You're not going in, West. I'll have a surveyor up from the camp to run the end line across, and get the distance to the Shoshone shaft; then I'll get underground, somehow, with a pocket compass."

"You'd better let me go down, sir."

"It can't be done that way. I've got to

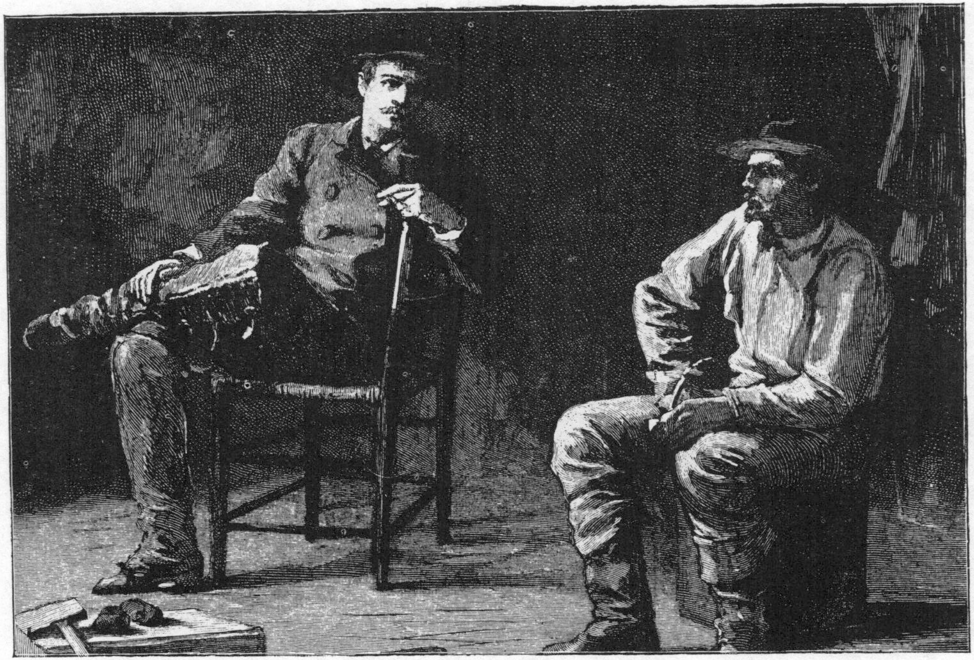

THE LED-HORSE IN COUNCIL.

give my affidavit to get out the injunction on.
Then we 'll drive that drift through, till we
can swear what ground we 're on ! "

" It 's a good time to go in now, sir. Conrath 's over the range, and Gash has been on
a spree. He won't be underground to-morrow,
anyhow. How much time would you want ? "

" I shall not go in until Conrath is back."
Hilgard had risen and stood before the fire,
his head well lifted, his cigarette burning out
in his fingers.

" I think you might 's well take your chance,
sir. He 'd do it with you, quick enough. It 's
no fool of a job you 're undertakin', Mr. Hilgard."

" I know it, West ; but, if I do it at all, I 've
got to do it my own way — not Conrath's way,
or Gashwiler's. I 'll take my chances with
Conrath on the ground."

IV.

THE YOUNGER SONS' BALL.

THE " Younger Sons " celebrated their fortnightly ball that evening in the dining-room
of the Colonnade House; the only suggestion
of a Colonnade in connection with the house
being the row of hitching-posts embedded in
the dried mud of the street before it.

The " Younger Sons " was a select bachelor
club, of the highest social aspirations. The
sons were not all in their first youth. Some of
them, it is to be feared, had known moments
which were not those of aspiration; but, as
sons go, they represented a tolerable filial
average. There might have been something
deprecatory in the modest title they had
chosen; at all events, they had found favor
with the indulgent mothers of the camp, who
accepted their invitations, and danced with
them at the fortnightly ball, with the assumed
approbation of the fathers.

Hilgard could have been a "Younger Son" had he desired. He had complimentary tickets sent him for the dances, for which unusual attention he was indebted to feminine, if not to maternal, influence. Men were at a discount on these occasions. They stood about in one another's way, and trod on one another's toes, against the wall, in a dreary, superfluous manner, which would have touched the sympathies of women not already overburdened with masculine claimants for them. Hilgard, having been gratuitously chosen as an object of feminine sympathy, would doubtless not have been sent to the wall; but heretofore he had been an unresponsive and ungrateful object. He had given away his ball-tickets, and his dress-suit had remained folded in the bottom of his trunk. To-night, however, at half-past nine o'clock, a visitor who stepped in out of the fresh night-air found him sitting at his office-desk, in full evening costume, writing telegrams.

It was a young lawyer of Hilgard's acquaintance, who, after a careless greeting, regarding him critically from a comfortable vantage in front of the fire, remarked, —

" Rather more style than the occasion calls
for, but you will do very well."

" What occasion?" Hilgard inquired, folding his telegrams.

" A snug little supper at Archer's. It's
rather late to ask you; fact is, you were n't
included in the first deal. I asked Pitt to
meet two Chicago men, just in, but he's gone
back on me at the last minute. Have you
got something else on hand?"

" I'm going to the Prodigals'." This was the
painful perversion which the title of " Younger
Sons " had suffered, in unfraternal circles of
the camp. " I'm getting rather sick of this
crawling about underground. It's a comfort
to stretch one's legs, and get on a suit of
clothes that is n't decorated in relief with
candle-grease."

" Come and stretch your legs under Archer's hospitable board; you won't find any use
for them at the Prodigals! You can't get a
partner at this hour. Every card in the room
is full."

" I may not dance, but I'm going. Shall I
send you a substitute?"

" If you can find me a good one; but you'd

much better come yourself and eat some trout. The Chicago men will think from your get-up that Led-Horse stock is booming. I won't tell them your ore is chiefly in the Shoshone bins."

As the legal counsel for the Led-Horse, intimately acquainted with its difficulties, Wilkinson might have been pardoned this jest; but Hilgard flushed, as he replied, —

" My get-up was not furnished by the Led-Horse. There is not much of the boy left in me, but I'm going to give what there is a chance to-night. To-morrow — " He repented, apparently, of having begun the sentence, and left it frankly unfinished, lifting his head and following with his eyes a ring of smoke that floated upward to the ceiling.

" To-morrow, you 'll bid good-by to youth forevermore, eh ? " Wilkinson remarked, eying the young superintendent with some amusement. " You 're expecting your gray hairs by the next stage ? "

" I'm expecting Conrath by the next stage. He is doing his best to promote my gray hairs."

" How are you getting on with your testimony ? " Wilkinson inquired.

"I'm going to hunt up some to-morrow. Confound it all, it's the worst mess you ever saw. We may have to appeal to the unwritten law, after all!"

"That's what you're doing to-night, isn't it, — with the Prodigals' ball for a tribunal? Conrath, I take it, isn't the defendant in this case!"

"I hadn't thought of retaining you for counsel, Wilke," Hilgard retorted. "What time is your supper?"

"Eleven, sharp. The Chicago men want to take in the town a little before they eat."

The two young men rode back to the camp together, and separated at the telegraph office. Hilgard did not enter the ball-room at once, but reconnoitred the scene from the office of the hotel, which communicated with it. Those who were not called to the feast were apt to congregate here, and pick up a few festal crumbs on the threshold.

Hilgard felt roused without being particularly happy. He was not analyzing his mood, or his right to dedicate these few hours, on the eve of an arduous struggle, to his personal claims. He was simply satisfying himself as to whether his fair neighbor of the Shoshone persuasion was among the dancers. Failing to discover her, he stepped within the doorway for a better view, and found himself just behind a lady of his acquaintance, who was participating in the old-fashioned quadrille, then in progress. He was about to change his position when she saw him and began to talk to him in the pauses of her facile performance.

She was a lively little matron, whose six months' residence in the camp made her a veteran in its society. In spite of a childish face, and light, inconsequent manner, she looked no longer young. The subtle change was like a premature blight on a still full-veined flower. Her youthfully rounded cheek had a slightly crumpled texture, and her eyes, of the blue of childhood, were too widely, restlessly expanded.

" What has brought you here at last, you incorrigible hermit? Or rather, *who* has brought you? You have not deigned to come and dance with us married ladies, — but no sooner " — she was " balancing " to one of the peripatetic partners in " Gentlemen to the

left!" and now she was whirled by the tips
of her fingers, and finished the sentence, looking at Hilgard over her shoulder as she received the advances of the next — "no sooner
do we boast of a lovely young girl from the
East, but you are here."

She whirled with Number Two, and continued, with her eyes still on Hilgard, as she
turned to Number Three, —

"But you are too late for anything but an
introduction. It serves you quite right."

Her partner now seized her by both hands,
and she was swept away in the final " Prome-
nade all!"

Hilgard moved on among the ranks of
black-coated wall-flowers, but encountered her
again as the quadrille broke up. She slipped
easily from her late partner's arm to his, and
addressed him with the utmost animation,
which yet missed, somehow, the full accent
of gayety.

"Why don't you ask me to introduce
you?"

"To whom, if you please?"

"Ah, what a fraud you are! I can see
your eyes wandering about everywhere in

search of her. You need n't pretend that you
don't know who I mean!"

"I suppose you are talking of your lovely
young girl from the East,—but how am I to
tell her from the married ladies?" said Hilgard, gazing around in mock bewilderment.

"That's very pretty of you, Mr. Hilgard.
I see you are trying to make your peace with
me. You know very well that you are talking to her chaperone."

"Am I, indeed?" Hilgard exclaimed, looking down into the upturned face of this guar-
dian of inexperienced youth. "What a fearful
responsibility! You look quite worn with it
already! Could I possibly be of any assistance to you in your duties?"

"Not the very least, I thank you; I have
been enthusiastically assisted already. She's
having a perfect 'ovation.' I must say she
keeps her head very well for a girl who has
been out so little."

"Do you suppose a young girl from the
East would call this being 'out'?" Hilgard
asked, indifferently. He was quite sure that
Mrs. Denny could not possibly be the chaperone of the young girl he had come to see,

and was very little moved by this picture of
her as a successful candidate for the social
honors of the camp.

"Well, I don't know what you would call
being 'out,' if this is n't! A perfect wealth
of partners, and so cosmopolitan! Why, a
girl could dance with a man from every State
in the Union!"

Hilgard had never felt a greater distaste
for the society of the little person who had
so freely bestowed herself upon him, than
to-night. He wondered why he did not escape from her. There was a fatality about
women of this kind, he had observed, and
vaguely questioned whether, as related to
social brutality in man, they represented cause
or effect.

Mrs. Denny at this moment leaned from
his arm with a smile of recognition to a young
lady who passed them with the circling promenaders. Her complexion exhibited a rather
weather-beaten fairness; her dry, lifeless yellow hair covered her forehead to her eye-
brows; the sleeves of her black satin dress
were cut very high on the shoulders, giving
her the appearance of a perpetual shrug.

Her throat and wrists were painfully small, and the hand which fluttered a passing greeting with her fan, had a meagre, attenuated expression in pathetic contrast to its gay gesture.

"Is that your young girl from the East?" Hilgard asked, carelessly.

"Mercy, no! Lou Palmer came from the East ten years ago! Lou has had a beautiful time, but she begins to show it a little."

"Is a 'beautiful time' so disastrous in its effects?"

"Well, perhaps Lou has had rather too good a time," said Mrs. Denny, with a reflective air.

"Here is the cynosure!" Hilgard began, then stopped, lifting his head with a quick, characteristic movement, and nervously touching his mustache. In the presence of the girl who stood before him, the light comment died on his lips.

The little crowd of "Younger Sons," which had indicated the force of some central attraction, had parted suddenly, allowing the undoubted object of their homage to pass. She had apparently distinguished none of

4

them with her favor, and her eyes had rather
a dazed absence of expression, as she came
toward Mrs. Denny.

It was Conrath's sister,—the fair Shoshone,
in the white shimmer of her maiden bravery;
her freshness undimmed by the warm, dusty
air of the ball, or its miscellaneous homage!

She glanced at Hilgard with doubtful recognition. Then, perceiving the identity of
this splendid youth with the clay-covered
knight of the prospect-hole, she gave him a
slight, cold greeting; too cold for the blush
that flamed, like a danger-signal, in her
cheek. She proudly repudiated the traitor-
ous color, however, and met his brilliant gaze
a moment, quietly, as a lady may.

"I need not introduce you, I see," observed
the astute chaperone. "You know Mr. Hilgard, Miss Conrath. He has not honored our
poor little dances until to-night. You must
help to insure his coming again."

The next dance was forming on the floor.
Hilgard, leaning against the whitewashed wall,
reckless of his black coat, found himself forgetting all the incongruities of the meeting in
the satisfaction it gave him. It was incon-

ceivable that she should be there, in her flow-
erlike brightness, among all these warped or
stale humanities. Conrath's admiration of
Mrs. Denny was no secret in the camp, but
that he should expect his young sister to
share it seemed incredible. It was more
probable that he had sacrificed his sister's
tastes to his own.

However, there she was, and she would be
there but a moment! Already, her partner
for the dance was industriously searching for
her among the promenaders and the groups
along the wall. Hilgard made use of his
height and breadth of shoulder to defeat this
search in an unobtrusive way. He was looking
down on the circle of lamplight which rested
on the top of the young girl's head, crossed
by a soft line of shadow where the maidenly
parting sank out of sight. The drooping,
rosy face, turned a little away from him, was
in shadow, too, and the small ear, innocent
of jewels, glowed as pink as a baby's, warm
from the pressure of the pillow.

Her petulance of their first meeting, when
she had lost her equanimity as well as her
way, was quite gone; the shy alarm of her

late greeting had also changed to a soft, surprised air of doubtful confidence, as if among
the many alien faces around her she had
found in his, so lately repelled, an unexpected, bewildering sympathy. She looked
at him again and again, with the brief, won-
dering glance of a child lost in a crowd,
whom some unknown friend has taken by the
hand.

Hilgard felt suddenly, deeply sobered. The
excitement in his blood, which had been gathering with the thickening plot of his troubles,
— which had driven him here to-night, — cli-
maxed suddenly in her presence. It strung
his rich, young voice to the lyric pitch, con-
trolled by the effort not to meet too eagerly
her hesitating preference.

"I wonder if you like a triumph of this
kind as much as most girls?" he asked; and
felt at once that the question was half an
insult.

"Is this a triumph?"

"Oh, no, not this," Hilgard went on desperately, with too keen a perception of the
briefness of the passing moment, "but what
I have just deprived you of."

"Do you imagine that I liked *that?*" looking at him reproachfully.

"You cannot have anything better than the best the place affords. May I see your card a moment? I shall not even go through the form of asking you for a dance. I only want to satisfy myself that you really have the best." He detached the pendent tassel from her bracelet, where it had caught. "Yes," he said, after a moment's grave perusal, "it is a proud record! The flower of the camp have hastened to enroll themselves. I should have been too late an hour ago!"

The inevitable partner was now very warm, indeed, on his quest, and it was no longer possible to frustrate his claims.

Skirting along the wall, fanned by the circling wings of the waltz, Hilgard joined an acquaintance seated in a quiet corner, near the door, — a well-preserved Younger Son, with a fresh-colored face and a humorous, uncertain, exaggerated expression, as if the facial muscles had become weakened in their action, like the keys of a long-used piano. His very respectable name of Thomas Godfrey had been for many years ignored gener-

ally by his friends, in favor of the gratuitous
title of Doctor. When applied to him, it
became, somehow, a familiar and affectionate, rather than a dignified, sobriquet.

"Doctor," said Hilgard, "do you want to
be an instrument of fate to-night?"

"Of whose fate, George? I've been an
instrument of my own fate for fifty odd
years; — the result does n't encourage me to
meddle with anybody else's."

"You have n't been passive enough. To-
night there is a chance for you to be perfectly
passive. You 've only to change places with me
for a few hours, — or let me change with you."

"Heaven forbid!" Godfrey interrupted.
"Do you call that being passive?"

"Wait till you hear me. It's a better
bargain than you think. I'm too late for a
dance, but you can have my supper at Archer's for one of yours, if you'll give me my
choice of your partners."

The Doctor fixed Hilgard sternly with his
heroi-comic gaze. "I understand your little
theory. Passivity for other folks, while you
keep rustling! How many men have you
made this offer to before you fell upon me?"

"Doctor, it is open only to you," said Hilgard, with a magnanimous air.

"Perhaps you're in collusion with some young lady in the room — I would n't be surprised! You've been studying her card and picked me out, between you, as the most gullible man on her list. George, I'm amazed at your impudence!" The Doctor meditated mournfully upon this quality in Hilgard, who appeared to be a favorite with him.

"Upon my soul, it's no conspiracy. I happened to see your name on a young lady's card, for a waltz — I know you can't waltz — you must have been out of your mind when you asked her — at this altitude! A good supper never comes amiss to a philosopher like you. I'm considering your interests as well as my own in this proposition."

"Thank you, boy. I'm capable of looking after my own interests, as yet. Out of my mind! At this altitude! Pray, have *you* tried waltzing at this altitude?"

"I've been waltzing up five hundred feet of pump-ladders, three days out of the week for the last six months, at this altitude."

"That's not to the point. I want to know

why I should n't propose to waltz with a nice girl as well as a thin-waisted young peascod like yourself! Do you suppose a man loses his gallantry as he gains in girth? George, I wish you had more stability of character!"

"I've got too much;— that's the trouble with me. I'm getting positively rigid. I came here to-night to limber myself up a little."

"Yes, you need limbering! Come — what is it you do want?"

"I want your waltz, Doctor, and you want my supper: you're hankering for it this minute — I can see it in your eye!"

"What, the supper? I can see it in *your* eye! I don't believe it exists anywhere else."

"Well — not at present, but it will exist at eleven o'clock. A three-handed spread with a dummy, — that is the way it stands now. Wilkinson asked me to take the place of dummy, in default of Pitt, delinquent."

"What was the matter with Pitt? What's the matter with you, — letting a good supper go begging round the camp? There must be something wrong about that supper. Trout, did you say?"

"Oh, yes. There's nothing the matter with Wilkinson's suppers, except the place where he has to give them!"

"Do you mean Archer's?"

"I mean the *place!* How can a man give anything in a place like this?"

"It's a good enough place, if you know how to take it. You're taking it too hard, my boy, — you're looking thin. Go and eat your own supper! You ought to be a valiant trencher-man at your age!"

"I'm a better waltzer than trencher-man."

"I don't believe you, George. You may be to-night, perhaps. A man's eye don't need to be as bright as yours to enjoy a good supper. It should grow a little tender — soften a little, as his spirit grows compassionate. What's the matter with you, boy? You look as I used to at your age, when I was getting into some awful scrape."

"Then you'd better keep me out of temptation and go to that supper in my place."

"Look here, George. It *was* a daring thing for me to do! — a man who hasn't waltzed for seven years."

"Seventeen, you mean, Doctor."

The Doctor placidly waved away the interruption.

" I 'll tell you how I came to do it.   Another man was just going to ask her, — a friend of Conrath's.   Con ought to be a little more circumspect in his friendships if he 's going to turn them all loose upon his sister."

" Well!" Hilgard interrupted impatiently.

" Well! I cut him out! Was n't it well done, at any risk, eh ?"

" It was like you, Doctor."

"No, it was n't at all like me. It might have been like me at your age — but now, look how I 'm weakening! I 'm rather inclined to take you up in that offer ! "

" Of course you are ! It 's a perfect arrangement : you defeat Conrath's friend, and reward yourself with a good supper."

" I 'm afraid you 're too anxious about my reward ; however, there 's a time for all things. You 're in the green tree and I 'm in the dry. When I was your age you would n't have got such a bargain out of me, though ! "

" Come, don't moralize. Eleven, sharp, is your hour. It will take you five minutes to put on your overcoat, and ten to find your hat."

" Well, good-night, boy. You're making a foolish bargain, but you'll be twenty years finding it out."

" I shall call it a very good bargain if it wears as long as that."

" You'll make my apologies to the young lady, George?"

" Trust me, Doctor! I'll do it as well as you could — at my age."

It is to be feared that Thomas Godfrey's apologies did not long dwell with those two fateful young souls, drifting so near to each other in the smooth involutions of the dance. Nor could the counter-charm of their crude and boisterous surroundings avail to reverse the spell, when its rhythmic circles were ended.

The candles in tin sconces against the wall burned dim, with long winding-sheets clinging to them. The lamps smoked in the draughts from the windows, let down to renew the morbid air of the room. As the waltz died, with a piercing bravura of the violins, the stage, belated on the pass, drove noisily up to the hotel entrance. Half the people in the room rushed into the office, or crowded around the doors, to witness the

disinterment of a file of bewildered passen·
gers from the damp, close interior of the
coach.

The cold night-air, tainted with a strong
smell of spirits, swept into the room with
the current of excitement. There were boisterous masculine greetings, loud laughter,
and the tramping of feet on the uncarpeted
staircase.

Hilgard and Cecil Conrath were together
in a corner of the half-deserted room. The
violins were tuning, and the heated trumpet-
ers, with their instruments under their arms,
were leaning from their chairs on the platform to accept glasses of refreshment handed
up to them from below. The young girl's fair
hair was slightly roughened, and its straying,
shining filaments caught the light; her gray
eyes, when the shy lids revealed them, looked
very dark, and the deepening color in her
cheeks was clearly defined by the whiteness
around her mouth.

"Are these from the aspens that grow in
our gulch?" Hilgard asked, looking down at
a cluster of pale yellow leaves that trembled
at her belt.

"Yes," she said, speaking with little breathless pauses, as the tide of the dance-music
ebbed in her breast. "I like them better than
the homesick-looking flowers the florists sell.
Do you enjoy things that seem to find it so
hard to live?"

"No, but I respect them," Hilgard replied.

"But we don't wear flowers out of respect
for them; and when there are so many painful
things in the world, — to have to sympathize
with flowers — "

She looked up for encouragement in her
generalization.

Hilgard's encouragement took the form of
a silent, unsmiling, downward look, and she
referred to her aspens again, rather hastily.

"These little leaves keep shivering in their
tough coats, but I believe it is a little affectation; they are really quite warm." She
shivered herself as she spoke.

"Is that a little affectation too?" Hilgard
asked.

"No, it is only somebody walking over the
place where my grave will be."

"Suppose you were destined to a sailor's
grave, — in the bottom of the sea."

"Then it might be a mermaid gliding past, you know, or a soft-footed seal." Again she gave a little quick shudder.

"It might be; but it is the wind, from that door. Let me fend it, so, with my shoulder."

She rested a moment against the wall in the shelter of the defensive shoulder.

"What is it the boys say when they play marbles?—'Fend' something," she asked, with fitful gayety.

"Fend dubs?" Hilgard suggested.

"Is it that? I thought it was something prettier!"

"Marbles was not a euphonious game when I played it."

"What does 'fend dubs' mean?" she persisted.

"I will teach you to play marbles, sometime, if you wish to learn," Hilgard said, with a deep, impatient inspiration, "but I think you fend very well."

They both laughed and then were silent, seeming to listen to a mental echo of the laugh, and of their light words. The young girl blushed despairingly at her own childish allusion. It sounded rough and slangy

to her, in the reproachful silence. The room
filled again, suddenly, and the open door was
shut. Hilgard resigned his protective attitude,
and moved farther away from her. He felt
impatient of the people crowding about them ;
they were helping to confuse those brief moments that lacked so little of perfection. It
was like trying to follow the faint thread of
a retreating melody through a maze of dis-
tracting sounds.

"I will never permit another aspen to be
cut on my side of the gulch." It was all he
could think of to say. "They shall be sacred
to you, from this evening."

"I wish you would let me tell you," she
began with a desperate courage, "how it was
I came — how I happened to be at the shaft
that morning."

"There was no reason why you shouldn't
be there."

"Yes, there was. A mine is private property. I know it was altogether queer. I saw
that you thought it was, then."

"I was perfectly delighted."

"But I was not there to delight anybody.
I simply thought I was on my brother's

ground. I was trying a new horse, and just wandering about anywhere."

" I 'm afraid I was rather impertinent. I was surprised, I confess, but it was the most charming surprise a man ever had in his life. Forgive me! What did I say to you that morning? Was I very offensive?"

" You were not quite — not as you are to-night."

" Not quite so offensive as I am to-night?"

" You are making fun of me!" she said, with a grieved upward look.

" I could not possibly make fun of you! But what can I say? You would not listen a moment to the things I want to say!"

She had been nervously fingering the cluster of leaves at her waist, and now one floated from its broken stem softly to the floor. He stooped for it, and held it as if it were a mutual confidence.

" I wish you would forget that morning," she said. " Make believe it did not happen!"

" If you choose to forget it — especially my part of it — I must not complain. But I 'm afraid I cannot spare it, unless you will promise me other mornings or evenings — better ones — to make up for it."

He was unconsciously proving a new range of looks, and tones which had been silent, heretofore, in the valiant procession of his years. It was the opening of the *vox humana* in his soul. The young girl listened to the "prelude soft"; she sighed, moving her head back restlessly, and with one hand crushing the limp plaitings of lace closer around her throat.

"There will be no more mornings or evenings," she said. "Everything I do here seems to be a mistake. This evening has been the worst mistake of all."

"I know what you mean. We are none of us living our real lives. But there might be perfect things, here, — perfect rides and walks and talks, — if one were not always alone, or worse than alone."

"But one always is!"

"But *need* one be? We are neighbors—"

"Yes," she interrupted, "you and my brother are neighbors! Oh, here is Mrs. Denny! I wondered if we were never going home!"

5

Mrs. Denny came toward them, between two gentlemen, laughing and shivering in a white cloak. Hilgard felt that the hovering joy of the moment had vanished.

" Did n't you hear the stage drive up, Cecil? Your brother is in at last. He says I may take you home with me to-night, and he will sleep at the hotel. He is completely done up — has n't even strength enough left to wonder how you got on without him to-night."

" Where is he?" Miss Conrath asked. " Cannot I go to him?"

" He is in bed by this time, my dear. He could scarcely stand on his feet."

" Is he ill ?" the girl inquired, anxiously.

" Of course he is n't ill!" Mrs. Denny smiled meaningly at Hilgard behind the young girl's back, and made a little wavering gesture back and forth with her small, wise forefinger. " Can't you imagine what twenty hours in that coach must be ?" she added.

" I don't need to imagine — I know!" Cecil said.

" Well, then! you cannot wonder he is fit for nothing but his bed!"

At the ladies' entrance — a recent addition to the Colonnade which could not be regarded as a triumph of privacy — Mr. Denny met them, and silently offered his arm to Miss Conrath, as if he had come for that purpose alone. He had spent the evening in a semi-detached state of attendance on his wife, varied by brief distractions of his own. Mrs. Denny gave him a quick, hard glance, when he first presented himself, perhaps to ascertain the nature of these distractions from their effects, but without altering her vivacity of manner.

V.

A PHILOSOPHER OF THE CAMP.

As Hilgard stepped into the street, his
brown mare, Peggy, swung around from the
hitching-post, and whinnied to him impatiently.
He patted her neck and rubbed her soft nose,
to console her for her disappointment, and
then, crossing the street, ran up a dark flight
of stairs to Godfrey's lodging.

He found the Doctor asleep in his arm-chair
before an air-tight stove that showed a red glow
at its draught.   The ashes of his cold pipe were
scattered over the ample bosom of his dressing-
gown, and a book had slipped to the floor beside
him.

"Eh ! what ?" he exclaimed, querulously,
arousing himself and feeling for a black silk
cap that had dropped from the bald spot on
the top of his reclining head.   "Is that you,
George ?   How did you get in ?"

" I saw a light under your door and heard you snoring, so I came in ; the door was unlocked."

" I snoring! Nonsense! I never unclose my lips when I sleep! What you heard was the roaring of the draught. Open that door, it 's very warm in here ! "

Godfrey leaned forward and closed the draught, then stretched himself back in his chair again, with a more benignant expression.

" Come, sit down, boy. Are n't your long legs tired enough yet, but you must go prowling about the room like that ? You 'll give me a crick in my neck, trying to see you over my shoulder."

Hilgard sat down on a low chair which brought his chin very close to his knees ; he rested his crossed arms on them and his chin on his arms, fixing his black-brown eyes on a crack in the stove through which he could watch the subsiding gleam of the fire.

" I hope you will sleep as well after your dance as I did after my supper," Godfrey remarked. His tone carried with it a certain perception of some mood in his young companion which might call for less careless hand-

ling than characterized their usual inter-
course.

"It strikes me it's time you were in search
of a bed somewhere. Did you come here to
share mine?"

"No, Doctor, — the fact is, you did me a
tremendous favor to-night."

"I rather suspected as much," the Doctor
assented, with a melancholy smile. He did
not look at Hilgard, but kept his eyes on the
stove. "George, I hope my pride in you is n't
going to have a fall."

"I hope not, Doctor," said Hilgard, indifferently; "but you had better put your pride in
a safer place."

"I 've gloried in your tough-heartedness
where woman is concerned, more than I have
in my own philosophy — eh?" added the
Doctor, in reply to some inarticulate comment
from Hilgard.

"With about as much reason, perhaps,"
George repeated.

"Don't be flippant, boy. It 's a pity you
can't take a lesson in the old man's philosophy, that you make light of at your own expense. Learn to inhale the delicate bouquet

and leave the wine alone, as I did at Archer's to-night."

The Doctor performed a fastidious gesture of lifting a fragile glass to his superior sense, closing his eyes in an ecstasy of appreciation.

"By the way," he went on, as Hilgard watched him, a hot impatience struggling with his usual enjoyment of the old boy's admonitions, "Wilkinson thinks he knows a good wine; perhaps he does; but if he does, then I don't! There isn't a wine in the place!"

He appeared to have lost the thread of his anxieties regarding the perilous state of Hilgard's emotions; but he presently returned to it, leaning back in his chair and closing his eyes, as having no one in view.

"All girls are pretty much alike when you get twenty or thirty years away from them — 'The brightest eyes that ever have shone,' you know, — what the deuce is the rest of it? I can't remember any poetry that I've read since I was ten years old. It's the essence a man wants in his life, not the individual flower; however, at your age I took a more specific view of flowers; I didn't object to one in my button-hole now and then."

"For Heaven's sake, hold on, Doctor!" Hilgard interrupted.

Godfrey put out a deprecating hand.

"Sit down, my boy, sit down. I understand you perfectly — no harm has been done so far. Your young legs ached for a dance with a pretty girl. Say *a* pretty girl — I don't insist on your dancing with more than one girl at once — whom you may never see again, and my chastened spirit yearned for an admirable supper. If I let my knowledge of young blood lead me into some foolish forebodings as to the future, why, that is n't to say that you 're bound to justify them."

Under the old boy's commonplace mannerisms of speech, and the whimsical play of his features, now growing a little heavy in their mobility, there was an accent of genuine tenderness. Hilgard, the boy of his recent fancy, understood him better than many of his oldest comrades, who had witnessed his slow deterioration, through twenty-six years of frontier life, and that series of postponed successes, roughly characterized by the world as failures, which had robbed him gradually of his youthful prestige among them. It was said of the Doctor that he was lazy, unambitious, and given to levity. A pervading seediness had crept over his outward man. The moth of long isolation from gentle communications had corrupted his good manners, and the thief of discouragement had stolen his pride. He sometimes consorted with the halt and the maimed in reputation; he did not always avoid the dark-colored sheep of the camp; but he was never known to be the companion of its birds of prey.

Hilgard was the only one of his acquaintance, perhaps, for whom he had any affection, who was not broken-winged, or weighted with some disability of character or fortune. His remnant of self-respect showed itself in his avoidance of the prosperous and flagrantly happy. He neither attempted to discount their successes, nor to share them; but for Hilgard, on the threshold of the fight, in his unstained armor and unquenched ardor of life, he felt all the yearning of a woman, with the doubts and fears of a disappointed man. This feeling expressed itself chiefly in gibes and grimaces of speech, which passed current between them much more easily than sentiments would have done.

" Your friend, Mrs. Denny," Hilgard began
after a silence, " in that delicate, arch little
way of hers, intimated that Conrath had been
drinking when he came in to-night. Is it a
habit with him, do you know ? "

" No, hardly a habit, as yet; a predilection,
perhaps. It 's a bad climate for predilections
of that kind."

" Do you suppose he — his sister has ever
seen him in that way ? "

" Heaven forbid ! No, to do Con justice, he
keeps himself out of the way when his little
predilection has got the upper hand of him.
He has ' important business down town.'
Women have a great respect for that. I 've
known Con's affairs to be so absorbing as to
keep him secluded for twenty-four hours at a
time, — trouble with the smelters, and what
not."

" Miserable, brutal business ! " Hilgard exclaimed, rising to his feet with a gesture
expressive of the general futility of things.
" Why is it that men who don't know how
to take decent care of a horse, always have
some woman at their mercy ? "

" Why, indeed, my boy, when chivalrous

hearts like yours and mine have n't so much as a rag of a favor to stick in our caps ! "

" What infernal selfishness to bring a girl like that out here, anyhow ! " Hilgard went on, without noticing the reckless inconsistency of the Doctor's present attitude with regard to feminine favors.

" Well, you and I should be the last to complain of that. The influence of a nice girl in a place like this, provided, mind you," said the Doctor, endeavoring to recover himself, " that no attempt is made to sequestrate the same —"

" And look at the friends he picks out for her ! " Hilgard interrupted passionately. " A rowdy little woman with a miscellaneous list of acquaintances — "

" Steady, my boy ! If you mean Mrs. Denny, — I'm one of Mrs. Denny's acquaintances, myself ! I knew her at Central before she was married. She was a bright-faced little thing just out of school. Family came from Tennessee — broken up by the war. Just fancy a girl beginning the study of human nature in a mining camp — and her own nature in the bargain. She began with Denny.

Are you listening to me, George ? I suppose
the only way for a woman really to know a
man is for her to marry him. If that's true,
in the course of an average life, with the
greatest perseverance, she could n't get very
far in the noblest study of mankind, could
she ? Well, Mrs. Denny knows Denny pretty
thoroughly, I suspect, by this time; and I
dare say she's been surprised at a good many
things she's found out in herself. Found
herself doing and saying and thinking a good
many things she never would have believed
herself capable of when she was a young girl.
She's a weak little vessel — the Lord knows
what she was fashioned for; but it was n't
for Denny — that I'll take my oath to. The
Lord never fashioned any woman for men like
Denny. She used to be very musical in a
chirrupy kind of way, but she does n't sing
any more — says she has n't any instrument.
If there's any music in that household, she's
the instrument and Denny's the player. It's
a wonder she is n't more out of tune. It
makes a ghastly kind of music in a family
when both have ceased to love, and one
knows how to torture."

" Doctor," said Hilgard, " I wish you would n't ! "

" Well, I won't — but you must n't, either ! Let her alone, poor little devil ! She is n't the kind that rebels and sets up her own individuality. I don't suppose she ever had much to set up. She just wobbles along, leaning a little too far one way and then a little too far the other, and Denny prods her up to her place now and then."

" What is the use of talking about it ? "

" Well, I won't; only look here — why should you grudge her the company of a sweet young girl ? If she can stand the contact, I should think the young girl might. Not that I 'd pick her out myself to matronize a girl of mine; but Conrath likes a lively little duenna, you see. By the way, George, — Conrath does n't seem to love you much. What 's the reason ? "

Hilgard looked uncomfortable.

" The reasons are underground — most of them."

" Some scrape about your end lines, I hear — "

" Yes."

" Well, that is n't all of it, is it ? "

" Is n't that enough ? "

" No, it is n't, in a camp like this. I 've known mèn to pocket each other's ore, and fight it out, and be on joking terms with each other, like 's not, half the time. You 're the one to feel ugly, it strikes me."

" Well, I do feel ugly."

" You don't feel as ugly as Con does, not by half. Come, I want to know what the trouble is ! "

Hilgard turned red.

" Hang it all ! " he said. " It 's that little fool of a woman you are trying to make me sorry for ! It began coming over the range. We made the trip from Fairplay together, Conrath and Mrs. D. and myself, and a lot more, shut up in that musty coach."

" You and Con made Mrs. Denny's acquaintance together, eh ? Well, that was an unlucky conjunction."

" Oh, he knew her before, and I did n't want to know her — "

" Ah ! " said the Doctor. " I see ! Well, it 's a pity. Mrs. Denny is a little fool, but not an inch of anything more."

"I don't care what she is, if she will only keep out of my way."

"You mustn't take up too much room with that way of yours, my boy. It's a small world. A fellow with as broad shoulders as you've got, can't go squaring them through it. We've got to turn out for the blind, and the lame, and the vicious. For your own sake, you'd better turn out for Conrath. He won't bear crowding. Give him plenty of room. I need n't tell you you'd better let his lady friends alone."

"I should think not, if you mean Mrs. Denny," Hilgard said, fiercely; "Conrath's lady friends are not likely to be mine."

"Well, his lady relatives, then. The sister is very nice and very pretty, but she belongs to the Shoshone crowd. You'll find it enough to be mixed up with them in business, without any sentimental complication."

Hilgard rose to his feet and straightened himself while he buttoned his overcoat, looking down at Godfrey with an expression of intense annoyance.

"Are you speaking of Miss Conrath?"

"Surely. Has Conrath more than one sister in the camp?"

"When you allude to a young lady as belonging to a 'crowd,' it is lucky for you, old boy, that it's not my sister you are talking about."

"I wish she were your sister. I'm going up to the Shoshone to-morrow," Godfrey added presently. "I want to look at that girl again. I can easily have some business with Conrath. Besides, I owe her an apology in person for the waltz last night."

"You'd much better keep away. You'll go up there with a bee in your bonnet, and make yourself ridiculous. She has forgotten which of us she waltzed with, by this time."

Hilgard had got as far as the door, but stopped and began walking up and down the shadowy part of the room while he expostulated with the Doctor.

"If you'll promise to keep away, I will," the latter called to him from the depths of his chair. "You are much safer and in better company with a ridiculous old fellow with a bee in his bonnet, than with any of that crowd. I say it again, whoever it offends!"

"Doctor, you are as bad as a dime novel. I could laugh, if you didn't make me so mad, at the wild absurdity and the cheek of you!"

"Well, 'some will laugh while others weep,'" said Godfrey, rubbing the black silk cap about, sleepily, on the top of his head. "Have you any idea how late it is? The respectable part of the camp has been in bed these two hours!"

Hilgard took no notice of this hint.

"Conrath can't be all rascal," he said, after a silence. "There must be a decent side to him if one could only get at it. How is that, Doctor, do you know?"

"I don't think he is a many-sided youth," Godfrey answered. "I 've seen only two sides of him, — Conrath when he has been drinking and Conrath when he has n't. I have n't found either very attractive. He has never done anything yet, but I 'm afraid when he cuts his wisdom teeth, he 'll cut them in iniquity."

Hilgard continued his perambulations in silence. A smouldering stick fell in the stove, and the flames started up again with a dull roar.

"Con," said the Doctor — "no, — George,

6

—don't you get too fraternally anxious about Conrath's sister." The Doctor's thoughts were evidently wandering. "Mrs. Denny's — little discrepancies — quite on the surface. Even — guileless observer like myself can perceive them." The words came lingeringly, with somnolent pauses. "I'm sorry — Con isn't better — boy — for her sake — Cecil's sake — and yours."

The black silk cap fell off, as the wearer's head, sagging from side to side, dropped back against his chair; his hand, with the pipeful of cold ashes, sank lower and lower, and rested on its broad arm. Hilgard picked up the cap, and pressed it quietly on the defence- less crown, which, as the Doctor said, had "got above timber-line."

"G' bless you, George. Go to bed, foolish boy!" the sleeper murmured.

VI.

BOUNDARY MONUMENTS.

THE Doctor's apprehensions with regard to Hilgard survived the night and clouded his enjoyment of a late breakfast, cooked by himself. He tried in vain to recall the face of the partner whom he had resigned, in a weak moment, to his favorite. He could only remember that she was young, with a sweet voice and fair, indefinite coloring. Surely there had been nothing about her that need have been irresistible, even to four-and-twenty. Reflecting, however, upon the position, relatively, of the two mines, and the dangers of propinquity and isolation combined, the Doctor resolved that he would take his threatened ride up to the Shoshone in the afternoon, and satisfy himself as to the potency of Miss Conrath's charms and the consequent extent of Hilgard's peril.

He inquired for Conrath, and was not surprised to find that he was not at the mine.
The Doctor had assured himself of that fact
before leaving the camp. Miss Conrath was
at home, however; on his asking to see her,
the maid showed him into the long, bright
room, with windows at both ends which served
for all the social uses of the managerial estab-
lishment. The young lady looked up from
her low seat by the hearth, in evident surprise,
at his entrance.

She appeared to have been sitting a long
time by the fire, for one cheek was quite hot
and red, and her lips showed a dry, vivid
brightness. She gave him a somewhat per-
functory welcome, as if, as a matter of course,
he had come to see some one else.

He began to realize, with some uneasiness,
that Conrath's sister was not quite such a
child as he had thought her to be. But
the Doctor had not the fear of woman, however young and fair, before his eyes. He referred at once to the ball, and to the waltz,
with the unblushing protestation that his
unavoidable rudeness had cost him his night's
rest.

Miss Conrath was not pleased with her visitor, but she was willing to bear with him for civility's sake. She was curious about him, too.

She was looking a little heavy-eyed and feverish after the ball. She had slept ill at Mrs. Denny's, and had not been able to compose herself to rest since her early return to the mine. But as the Doctor looked at her he was more and more disgusted with his own fatuity of the night before.

He almost groaned as he studied her, and saw how more than pretty, how adorable, she was!

She sat somewhat listlessly engaged with a mass of soft white knitting she had unfolded from a silk handkerchief which she spread across her lap, while the Doctor discussed the chances of the railroad getting through to the camp before winter, and indulged in the usual revilings of the climate.

"Did you ever have the asthma, Miss Conrath?" he asked, pursuing this theme with variations.

"I don't remember that I ever did," Cecil laughed. She was able, as yet, to regard illness, connected with herself, as a kind of joke.

"Well, I dare say you never did. But then, you know, even babies have been known to have it. Well, this is the most marvellous climate for asthmatics, in fact, for any kind of chronic complaint. But I've observed these stimulating climates that stir old blood out of its torpor are the very — are a — all wrong for healthy youngsters. Young blood don't require a light atmosphere any more than it requires a whiskey-and-soda — if you will excuse me — every morning before breakfast. I don't know, upon my soul, how else to account for the way all the young fellows go to the deuce out here."

Cecil looked up at her visitor in great surprise. She thought he might possibly be approaching the subject of a hospital or free reading-room, or course of lectures for young men, with a view to asking for contributions; but he did not look like an agent for a benevolent enterprise. She was at a loss to understand the turn he had given to the conversation.

The Doctor certainly was taking a most

extreme view of his duty in this situation, which he had found so much worse than could have been expected. There was no doubt as to Hilgard's symptoms. They had been of a nature calculated to shake far more than the Doctor's boasted faith in his tough-heartedness. He had no objection to the young lady. A perfect lamb, he said to himself, and yet with a spirit of her own in those steady gray eyes, under the wide low arch of the soft eyebrows. But she was allied to a masculine element in the camp, the nature of which the Doctor understood better than Hilgard. It was evident that his warnings had been thrown away on that headstrong youth. He must see what could be done with the fair Shoshone. There was no way left but to traduce Hilgard — blacken his character — deal with him remorselessly, and make her afraid of him. George might think the treatment of his symptoms a little rigorous, but he would live to be thankful for it. The Doctor would shrink from nothing, where the safety of his "boy" was concerned.

"He can talk about his dime novels," he soliloquized gloomily, "but the state of things

here is not much better. It's mediæval,—
that's what it is!"

"There's that young Hilgard," he began
violently. As if the word had been a blow,
the color answered in the young girl's cheek.
She had expected that name some time in the
course of the conversation, but was not prepared for it in this connection. "George
Hilgard was a perfect specimen of young
manhood when he first came from the East;
he was like Saul among his brethren."

The unhappy blush deepened until it had
quite obliterated the fire-glow.

"I don't know what can have got into that
boy, unless it's the altitude! He needs more
atmospheric pressure — the more pounds to
the square inch the better for a chap like that.
I've been foolish enough to let in a sneaking
kind of a fancy for that young limb, but, upon
my soul, if he's got any friends in the East,
they'd better send for him! They'd better
get him out of this camp!"

The young girl looked steadily at her work
without speaking, while a paleness about her
lips spread slowly backward over her cheeks.

"I'm sure I don't know what time he got

to bed last night! He came tramping up my stairs long after midnight to talk over his troubles with me. I knew he was getting into some scrape or other! That boy has got to get out of the camp!"

The Doctor concluded, from the victim's expression, that he had gone far enough. He had not, indeed, intended to go quite so far, but the effort his words had cost him had given them an impetus which surprised himself. Miss Conrath's head was bent very low over her knitting, and the white wool slid over her fingers with a fitful, uncertain movement. He now proceeded calmly to give his remarks a more general tendency.

"That's a very pretty thing you're working on, — looks as white and soft as a fresh snowfall. Hope it will keep white longer than the snow does that falls in this dusty camp."

With her needle between her tremulous fingers, Cecil held out the corners of the handkerchief.

" I keep it folded in this," she said.

" Ah, yes," the Doctor murmured abstractedly, " that's a good way, too! Ridiculous idea for an old fellow like me to be dwelling on; but if I had a young sister or daughter in this camp, I dare say I should be inclined to keep her as you keep your white wools — folded away from the dust."

He paused a moment, awaiting some comment from Miss Conrath. But none came; she took a long breath and rested her arms on her lap, looking down into the fire. The Doctor derived great satisfaction from her attitude, and the long sigh, as of one who rests a moment after pain.

She began to wince — poor little thing! He would give one more turn to the screw and then let her breathe again. It was absolutely necessary that she and Hilgard should not be running across each other at balls, every fortnight or so. George would easily find means to re-establish himself in her eyes, if he had the chance. The Doctor would do what a devoted friend might, to deprive him of that chance.

"Now, that ball of the 'Younger Sons,'" he went on; "they claim to be very exclusive, poor fellows! I'm one of them myself, so far as the name goes, but I don't pride myself on it. A younger son is no better than an older one,—sometimes not half so good. What did you think of the ball, Miss Conrath? Did it strike you as being very exclusive?"

Miss Conrath lifted her eyes a moment, but without looking at the Doctor.

"I do not think those who went to the ball are the ones to criticise it," she said.

"Surely not," the Doctor cordially assented; "but, on the other hand, those who did not go are hardly the ones! You and I have been, Miss Conrath; and, if I may judge by your expression, rather than your words, you find yourself not quite acclimated to the pitch of gayety required to enjoy a camp ball."

"My brother was not there, as I expected," Cecil protested.

"Ah, yes, of course that makes a difference; but it makes more difference here than it would anywhere else. Here, there is no classification. You have to pick your way among all the people who are crowding you, elbow to elbow. What is a young girl to do? You are no judge of character, Miss Conrath. I hope you are not, at your age. You are perfectly defenceless here, the moment you get outside your door. So is any young girl."

Miss Conrath rose suddenly, as if her endurance had reached a limit.

"It is true," she said, "I must be defenceless, when strangers give themselves the right to take my brother's place — and in his own house."

The Doctor rose, too, smiling at her with invincible composure. He was well satisfied with the effect of his desperate measures. To make all sure for the future he would not spare the final blow.

"Neither Hilgard nor I dared to be perfectly frank with you about that exchange of partners last night. Shall I make a clean breast of it and tell you the facts?" he asked.

Cecil faced him, her soft eyes expanded with a pained brightness.

"I will hear nothing more; you have been too frank already," she exclaimed, indignantly. "Please to have some regard for me, if you have none for your friend. I have heard things to Mr. Hilgard's discredit from others who did not profess to like him, but it is his friend who has no mercy on his character, and no respect for his confidence."

The Doctor was instantly and mightily roused at the thought of these "others," less disinterested detractors, at work upon Hilgard's character. His was the only hand that could be trusted to administer the blackening touches, and even his began to tremble remorsefully at the picture he had faintly sketched of his boy, a prey to the cheap temptations of the camp. He sat down again, bent on investigating this unexpected aid which had anticipated him in the work of defamation.

"I should like to know," he burst forth, "who has been warning you against George Hilgard! Perhaps your brother has been enlarging on him for your benefit. You needn't pay the least attention to that sort of thing. Your brother and Hilgard are engaged just now in a discussion of their boundary lines. Half the mines in the camp are doing the same thing; their opinion of each other is likely to be more picturesque than edifying. What has your brother got to say about Hilgard?"

"I have not mentioned my brother's name!"

"Of course you haven't. You appear to

have more sense than most girls; but you
may take my word for it, Miss Conrath, that
when you hear anything to the discredit of
George Hilgard, it's invented by the person
who brings it to you, I don't care who he
is! Of course, your brother has got to keep
Hilgard at a distance. The chief of the
Led-Horse can't be chasseing back and forth
across the gulch with the sister of the Shoshone! You can't be putting a man's ore in
your pocket with one hand and asking him to
dinner with the other."

" Mr. Godfrey!"

" Oh, I know I'm in your brother's house.
I'm only expressing the general sentiment
down in the camp. *I* don't know anything
about their squabbles! I only know that
George Hilgard's the finest young fellow in
this camp. He'd be one of the ten who
would save the city, if we could find the other
nine!"

" I don't know whom you are defending him
from. You yourself have said the worst
things," Cecil protested.

" What have I said? I said he was in
trouble. So he is! So he is! Or if he isn't,

he's in a fair way for it. It's easy enough
to see the beginning," — he looked mena-
cingly at the bewildered girl, — " but there
is no telling where it will end! I've done
what I could. There's not a young fellow
living for whom I'd have done what I've
done for him to-day! But I give it up!"
The Doctor spread out both his palms with
a hopeless gesture.

Cecil began to feel a little afraid of her
eccentric visitor, who did not seem to be out
of his mind, nor yet altogether in it. She
was troubled by a suspicion that he must
have some motive for his grotesque outburst
of confidence with regard to Hilgard. She
could hardly take it as a wanton imperti-
nence toward herself.

" I must ask you to excuse me from any
more discussion of your friend. What he is
or is not, cannot concern me. My brother
will be at home soon, I think, if you like to
wait for him."

She felt that her discourtesy had been well
deserved, and, without further apology, she
left the room.

The Doctor remained sitting for some time

alone; he looked down at the prints of his dusty feet on the carpet, then at the heap of white knitting the girl had dropped. " Well! if women are n't the very — "

At that moment the maid entered with a jingling tray of glass and silver, which she proceeded to arrange on the sideboard at the farther end of the room. The Doctor took out a card and scribbled a few words on it.

" Will you give this to Miss Conrath ? " he said, handing it to the maid. The words were : —

" Forgive me if I have made you uncomfortable. You need not remember anything I have said. Any inconsistencies you may have noticed in my remarks, I will commend to your charity for an old fellow who was kept up much too late the night before ! "

The Doctor was obliged to confess to himself, as he rode back to the camp, that the four dollars he had spent that afternoon for horse-hire were entirely thrown away, so far as it was ever likely to benefit Hilgard.

" It all comes of the missionary spirit," he grumbled to himself. " A man never goes out with that spirit on him, that he is n't sure to poke himself into some place where he's no business to be."

After sunset of the same day, Cecil Conrath was walking back and forth on the hillside above the gulch, following an unfrequented trail, screened by the quaking aspens from view on the side of the Led-Horse, and sheltered from the winds by the crest of the hill. The miners, observing that the young girl often walked here alone, had, with tacit courtesy, left this trail to her exclusive use.

To-day she ventured farther than usual into the gulch, attracted by the flutter of a red flag among the parting leafage. It was planted in the centre of a clump of young trees, aspens of larger growth, and slender, branchless pines growing in the bottom of the gulch. The ominous signal, awaiting some unknown issue in this lonely spot on the debatable ground between the two mines, gave Cecil a curious shock of apprehension. The air was full of rumors of incipient trouble. The situation had never been explained to her; she knew that Hilgard was the accuser and her brother the defendant, and that the affairs of the accuser were at a low ebb, while those of the defendant prospered amain; more than this, she had only her forebodings, which had not been allayed by the tone her brother invariably used in speaking of his neighbor.

Venturing nearer, she saw that the trees which stood around the signal flag were each defaced by the hacking of a large piece of bark from the trunk, and bore an inscription deeply cut in the white, exposed wood. The leafy covert, where the shadows, stealing down between the hills, made an early dusk, might well have served for a trysting-place; but these were no amorous records which the young girl deciphered, as she went from tree to tree, tracing the rude intaglio; unless, indeed, the lovers had concealed their mutual vows under an arithmetical formula.

The red flag drooped in the failing breeze. Cecil now observed that it was planted between two narrow, flat stones, partly driven into the ground, side by side; the stones bore the same mysterious formulæ with which the tree-trunks were branded.

What had happened in this secluded spot,

with these young trees standing about like mute witnesses, each bearing its scar for a token; and what coming event was this red signal beckoning on?

173300

She heard a man's footsteps striding rapidly down the trail behind her; she waited under the blazed trees until they should pass. They did not pass, but came near and paused, and Hilgard's voice, low, and a little disturbed by rapid heart-beats, gave her " Good evening."

" Is it very strange for me to be here?" she asked, instinctively summoning him to her own defence. " I never come down into the gulch; but I saw this flag from the hill. I could not think what it meant!"

His presence had changed her unaccountable panic into a definable dread lest, when she looked in his face, she should see there records, unobserved before, of that deterioration, or capacity for it, which Mr. Godfrey had ruthlessly depicted and then recklessly denied. She lifted her eyes doubtfully to his.

As if he felt the subtle question in them, his own met hers with their manly answer. It was enough, and more than enough. She had not asked for all the assurances that she read in his eyes.

" It is altogether so very strange here," she said, looking about restively at the encircling trees.

" Has anything frightened you, or troubled you ? "

" Oh, no — it is only the place. Why are the trees all cut and marked, and these little stones? What has happened here? Do you know ? "

Hilgard could not forbear a smile.

" Only a very little thing happened here a year and a half ago. The southwest corner of the Led-Horse and the southeast corner of the Shoshone were located here. The end lines of the two claims are identical. These stones are the corner monuments, and the number of the corner and of the official survey are marked on them and on the trees. Did it seem so very mysterious to you ? "

" I thought these stones marked the grave of some one buried here."

" The graves of a good many fortunes are marked by such stones as these. But they do not usually mean anything more tragic."

" And what does this flag mean ? "

" It has been used for a survey that was

made to-day along the line. The flag was placed here for what is called a ' back-sight,' to insure keeping the line ahead straight."

" Then it does not mean danger of any kind ? "

" I hope not, I am sure," Hilgard replied. "Are you a little sensitive, perhaps, about danger ? " he suggested, smiling.

" When one is alone a good deal one is apt to get morbid," she admitted.

He looked at her wistfully, thinking of his own loneliness, which he had not been conscious of until she became his neighbor.

" And the direction one's morbidness takes, depends on temperament, I suppose. My morbidness takes the direction of various kinds of happiness I might have, but never expect to," he said.

" I should think you might be quite happy in your little kingdom over there." Her clear accents struck with thrilling sweetness on the stillness.

" You will have a kingdom of your own some day. I hope you will like it better than I do mine."

She turned her cheek toward him, with a

movement of attention, but without looking at him.

"Will you tell me if I am on our side of the 'line'?" she asked.

"The Shoshone side, do you mean?"

"Yes, of course."

He came a few steps nearer to her. "Now we are both on the Shoshone side; you will let me stay on your side a moment, will you not?"

"But is that surveyor looking at the flag now?" she exclaimed, with a sudden accent of alarm at the thought of a mathematical instrument which might be of the nature of a telescope brought to bear on her under the present circumstances.

Hilgard reassured her by pulling up the "back-sight" and tossing it on the ground. The survey had been finished an hour ago, he explained; he had happened to remember the flag in passing, and had come to take it away.

She turned now toward the upward trail; but Hilgard, walking at her side, besought her to give him a few moments more.

"Am I never to see you," he asked, —

"as other people see you, — as I might see you anywhere but here? Why may I not walk with you now, up the hill to your brother's house? There is no personal feeling on my part, in this unpleasant business between the mines. You have heard of it, of course, but it need be only a business disagreement. Your brother and I should not be enemies!"

She had stopped as he overtook her, and now walked back irresolutely toward the group of trees.

"I hope you are not enemies!" she said. "It is so causeless! So — so — incredible! I do not understand what it is! No one has explained it to me. Could you tell me?"

"No," said Hilgard, dejectedly; "I am not the one to tell you. You must have what faith you can in — both of us — until the truth comes out. But it is very hard to feel that your strongest bias must always be against me. If you would give me but the merest chance that any acquaintance might have, to put myself in some other light than the one I am doomed to in your eyes. You will always think of me as a determined partisan of the wrong side."

"If my brother brings you to the house, I will think of you only as our guest."

"Is that likely to happen, do you think?" he asked bitterly.

"No," she said, "it is not at all likely, but there is no other way." She stood with her shoulder against a slender pine and looked down at the scar in its side, touching it with remorseful fingers. "I don't know why it should be so, but I have known from the first that there could be no softening of this — of the bitterness between you and my brother by any effort of mine. It is a woman's place always to make peace, but it has been useless to try."

"But I declare to you that there *is* no bitterness on my part."

"Wherever it lies, it is there!" she said. "We cannot be friends — or even acquaintances."

"But you cannot make me your enemy! The bitterness shall not include us! What a strange fate it is that I should be on any side that is not your side!"

She was already moving away, but, at his words, she looked back without speaking. In the gathering dusk he could not read the expression of her eyes, but the mute action, trustful yet forbidding, racked his self-control.

VII.

THE BARRICADE.

MRS. DENNY had won from Conrath a reluctant promise that he would take her down the main shaft of the Shoshone, and through its subterranean workings. He had postponed the fulfilment of this promise until it had become a subject for rather keen bantering between these lively comrades. On the second day after the ball, Conrath surprised Mrs. Denny by asking her if she was ready to go down in the mine that afternoon.

He had called at her house in the morning, and the plan had been discussed between them as he sat on his horse, and she leaned on the pine-pole railing of the porch, wrapped in one of the fluffy white shawls in which she was fond of muffling her small, chilly form. Conrath was looking pale and somewhat demoralized after his stage-ride and its contingencies, the nature of which Mrs. Denny had gracefully indicated by pantomime to Hilgard on the night of the ball.

Mrs. Denny considered Conrath very handsome, — almost as handsome as Hilgard, and far more appreciative and generally available. She protested that she could not endure the wind on the porch, and chid him for permitting his pony to nibble the young growth on her favorite clump of fir-trees; but she did not go in, and Conrath lingered, as if he had something on his mind which he found it difficult to say.

"That beastly coach makes a perfect imbecile of a man," he began, with more vigor of expression than the uncertain look in his eyes bore out; "I felt, when I got in on Wednesday night, as if I had been kicked from Fairplay over the pass."

"Oh, I saw you," she replied, with a teasing smile. "It was plain enough that something had mixed you up pretty well! I told your sister you were a perfect wreck, — could n't stand on your feet; was n't that true?"

"Did you tell her that?"

"Of course I did. What was she to think of your leaving her at loose ends that way for

the night? Who was to take her up to the
mine? You 're a nice brother, I must say!
She was a great deal more anxious about you
than you deserved. She wanted to go to you,
but I kept her away, — more for her sake
than yours!"

Conrath flushed and laughed, with an awkward pretence of being amused at these ac-
cusations.

"I don't know who is to answer for all the
fibs I had to tell her," Mrs. Denny continued;
"you can't, because your time for repentance
is fully occupied, — or ought to be!"

Conrath, shifting uneasily in his saddle,
regarded Mrs. Denny's audacity with sulky
admiration. It gave a certain piquancy to the
commonplace nature of his weaknesses to be
rallied upon them by a pretty woman.

"Are you sure Cecil did not know how it
was the other night?" he asked.

"Do you suppose I would tell her?"

"No, but plenty of other people might.
She has been very quiet and — well, different
since the ball."

"You are very fond of your sister, are n't
you, Con?"

"Of course I am. Why should I have brought her out here if I was n't fond of her?"

"To be sure; that is proof enough." Mrs. Denny laughed her little mocking laugh. "She must be very fond of you, or she would n't have come. How does she amuse herself up at the Shoshone?"

"Well, she is alone a good deal, but she is used to that. She walks, and reads, and looks at the mountains. She could ride, if I ever had time to go with her."

"Con, when your sister has been out here a year she won't need any information I or any one else could give her about you. She will know you thoroughly; she will think you all out. I wonder if she will have as much faith in you then as she has now?"

Conrath looked at Mrs. Denny uneasily. "Are you preaching?" he asked. "Or what is it you are trying to get at?"

"Does it sound to you like preaching? If you can find a sermon in it, you are welcome. Much good may it do you!"

"Cecil is not as clever as you think," Conrath said, as if still considering Mrs. Denny's words. " She is n't cool and sharp, like you, and she is n't one of the exacting kind."

" *Is n't* she!" Mrs. Denny exclaimed. "Not in the way of attentions, perhaps; but if she should come to judge you once as she judges herself — "

Conrath's horse began to be restive.

" Are you trying to make me afraid of my little sister?" he interrupted.

" You might make her your conscience," Mrs. Denny replied. " It is n't a bad thing for one to be a little bit afraid of one's conscience."

" You seem to have my failings on your mind — you might be my conscience yourself," Conrath suggested, — " taking it for granted, of course, that I have none of my own."

" No, thank you. You will need to keep your conscience nearer home. Besides, I might be too lenient."

Mrs. Denny laughed, and ran into the house.

The party set out for the shaft-house after the three-o'clock whistle for the change of shifts had blown. The ladies were wrapped

in india-rubber cloaks, and Mrs. Denny wore
a soft felt hat of Conrath's on the back of her
head, framing her face and concealing her
hair. A miner's coat was spread in the bucket
to protect the visitors' skirts from its muddy
sides.

" If we keep on shipping ore at this rate,"
Conrath said, jubilantly, " we will soon have a
cage that will take you down as smoothly as
a hotel elevator."

Cecil was conscious that the exultant tone
jarred upon her, and she took herself silently
to task for this lack of sisterly sympathy.

Mrs. Denny went down first with the superintendent, who returned for Cecil; when they
were all at the station of the lowest level,
they lit their candles and followed one of the
diverging drifts, — a low, damp passage which
bored a black hole through the overhanging
rock before them.

The sides of the gallery leaned slightly
together, forming an obtuse angle with the
roof ; it was lined with rows of timbers placed
opposite each other at regular intervals, and
supporting the heavy cross-timbers that up-
held the roof. The spaces between the upright

columns were crossed horizontally by smaller timbers called " lagging."

The impalpable darkness dropped like a curtain before them. Their candles burned with a still flame in the heavy, draughtless air. At long intervals a distant rumbling increased with a dull crescendo, and a light fastened in the rear of a loaded car shone up into the face of the miner who propelled it. They stood back, pressed close to the wall of the drift, while the car passed them on the tram-way.

The drift ended in a lofty chamber cut out of the rock, the floor rising at one end toward a black opening which led into another narrow gallery beyond.

" Here we are in the very heart of the vein," Conrath explained. " This is an empty ' stope,' that has furnished some of the best ore. It is all cleaned out, you see; the men are working farther on."

" Oh, I should like to see them!" Mrs. Denny exclaimed. " Which way is it? Up that horrible place? Cecil, are n't you coming?"

Cecil had seated herself on a heap of loose planking in the empty ore-chamber.

"I 'll wait for you here, if you don't mind; I am so very tired. Have you another candle, Harry?"

"Yours will last; we shall not be long gone."

Conrath and Mrs. Denny scrambled, talking and laughing, up the slope; their voices grew thinner and fainter, and vanished with their feeble lights in the black hole.

Cecil closed her eyes; they ached with the small, sharp spark of her candle set in that stupendous darkness.

What a mysterious, vast, whispering dome was this! There were sounds which might have been miles away through the deadening rock. There were far-off, indistinct echoes of life, and subanimate mutterings, the slow respirations of the rocks, drinking air and oozing moisture through their sluggish pores, swelling and pushing against their straitening bonds of timber. Here were the buried Titans, stirring and sighing in their lethargic sleep.

Cecil was intensely absorbed listening to this strange, low diapason of the under world. Its voice was pitched for the ear of solitude

8

and silence. Its sky was perpetual night, moonless and starless, with only the wandering, will-o'-the-wisp candle-rays, shining and fading in its columnated avenues, where ranks of dead and barkless tree-trunks repressed the heavy, subterranean awakening of the rocks.

Left to their work, the inevitable forces around her would crush together the sides of the dark galleries, and crumble the rough-hewn dome above her head. Cecil did not know the meaning or the power of this inarticulate underground life, but it affected her imagination all the more for her lack of comprehension. Gradually her spirits sank under an oppressive sense of fatigue ; she grew drowsy, and her pulse beat low in the lifeless air. She drooped against the damp wall of rock, and her candle, in a semi-oblivious moment, dropped from her lax fingers, and was instantly extinguished.

It seemed to the helpless girl that she had never known darkness before. She was plunged into a new element, in which she could not breathe, or speak, or move. It was chaos before the making of the firmament. She called

aloud, — a faint, futile cry, which frightened
her almost more than the silence. She had lost
the direction in which her brother had disappeared, and when she saw an advancing
light she thought it must be he coming in
answer to her weak call.

It was not her brother; it was a taller man,
a miner, with a candle in a miner's pronged
candlestick fastened in the front of his hat.
His face was in deep shadow, but the faint,
yellow candle-rays projected their gleam dimly
along the drift by which he was approaching. Cecil watched him earnestly, but did
not recognize him until he stood close beside her. He took off his hat carefully,
not to extinguish the candle which showed
them to each other. Cecil, crouching, pale
and mute, against the damp rock, looked
up into Hilgard's face, almost as pale as her
own.

No greeting passed between them. They
stared wonderingly into each other's eyes,
each questioning the other's wraith-like identity.

"I heard you call," Hilgard said. "Is it
possible that you are alone in this place?"

"No," she replied, feebly rousing herself. "My brother is here, with Mrs. Denny; they are not far away."

"Your brother is here — not far away?" he repeated. A cold despair came over him. There was nothing now, but to tell her the truth; in her unconsciousness of its significance she would decide between them, and he would abide the issue. He leaned against the wall of the drift, wiping away the drops of moisture from his temples; the short, damp locks that clung to his forehead were massed like the hair on an antique medallion.

"You did not know me?" he asked.

"No; I could not see your face."

"I am not showing my face here. I am a spy in the enemy's camp. Your brother will hear the result of my discoveries, in a few days, from my lawyers."

It was roughly said, but the facts were rough facts; and he could not justify or explain himself to her, except at the expense of her brother.

"Must I tell him that you are here?" she asked.

"I suppose so, if you are a loyal sister."

"But I would never have known it, if you had not come when I called. My candle fell and went out. I was alone in this awful darkness."

"But some one else would have come if I had n't. You need not be grateful for that. Your brother would have found you here."

"But I could not have endured it a moment longer!"

"Oh yes, you would have endured it. I need not have come."

"Why did you come, then?"

"I don't know," he said. "I was a fool to come. Why does a man come, when he hears a woman's voice, that he knows,—in trouble?"

He was groping about on the floor of the drift in search of her candle; and now, kneeling beside her, he lit it by his own and held it toward her. Their sad, illumined eyes met.

"How your hand trembles! Were you so frightened?" he asked.

"Yes; does it seem very silly to you? My strength seemed all going away."

It was madness for him to stay, but he could not leave her, pale, and dazed, and helpless as she was.

"Let me fix you a better seat." He moved the rough boards on which she was sitting, to make a support for her back.

"Oh, please go, and get out of the mine!" she entreated, — with voice and eyes, more than with words.

"But I cannot get out, until the next change of shifts. I have taken the place of one of the miners on this shift; besides, I have not finished what I came for."

"Why do you call yourself a spy? are you doing anything you are ashamed of?" she asked, with childlike directness.

"I am a little ashamed of the way I am doing it," he replied, with equal directness, "but not of the thing I am doing."

"And will it injure my brother — what you are doing?"

"Not unless the truth will injure him; I am trying to find out the truth."

"But why should you come in this way to find it out? Surely my brother wants to know it too, if it is about this quarrel."

It was a home question; he could only answer, —

"Your brother is very sure that he knows the truth already. *I* want to be sure, too. I am not asking you *not* to tell him I am here. I have taken the risks."

"What are the risks?" she asked quickly.

"They are of no consequence compared with the thing to be done — I must not stay."

"Ah," she cried, with an accent of terror, "they are here!"

A light showed at the dark opening above the incline, and the thin stream of Mrs. Denny's chatter trickled faintly on the silence.

Cecil put out both candles with a flap of her long cloak.

"Oh, *will* you go!"

Hilgard heard her whisper, and felt her hands groping for him in the darkness, and pushing him from her. He took the timid hands in his and pressed them to his lips, and then stumbled dizzily away through the blackness.

A proposition from her companions to prolong their wanderings until they had reached the barricade was opposed by Cecil with all the strength her adventure had left her; but when it appeared that their way lay along the same drift in a direction opposite that by which Hilgard had made his retreat, she offered no further objection. Her silence was sufficiently explainable by the fright she had had in the darkness.

The drift led to another smaller ore-chamber, where miners were at work, picking down the heavy gray sand, and shovelling it into the tram-cars. Conrath explained that this " stope " was in the new strike, claimed by the Led-Horse, and that the barricade guarded the drift just beyond.

" I suppose it does n't make so much difference whom the ore belongs to," Mrs. Denny commented lightly; " it 's a question of who gets it first! *Passez, passez!* You need n't stop to expostulate. I am not a mining expert."

Conrath looked excessively annoyed, but refrained from defining his position to this cheerful non-professional observer. As they entered the low passage, they found themselves face to face with a wall of solid upright timbering which closed its farther end, and in the midst of a silent group of men, seated along the side-walls of the drift on blankets and empty powder-kegs.

The barricade was pierced at about the height of a man's shoulders with small round loop-holes. Two miners' candlesticks were stuck in the timbers, high above the heads of the guard, who lounged, with their rifles across their knees, the steel barrels glistening in the light.

Cecil's fascinated gaze rested on this significant group. The figures were so immovable, and indifferent of face and attitude, so commonplace in type, that she but slowly grasped the meaning of their presence there. These, then, were the risks that were of no consequence!

Turning her pale face towards her brother, she asked, "Is *this* what you have brought us to see?"

"I thought you knew what a barricade is!"

"I never knew! I knew — I thought it was that," — pointing to the wall of timber — "but not this!" She looked toward the silent group of men, each holding his rifle with a careless grasp.

" You would n't make a good miner's wife, Cecil," said Mrs. Denny ; and a slow smile went round among the men.

" Hark," said Conrath. They were still facing the barricade, and the dull thud of picks far off in the wall of rock sounded just in front of them. " Do you hear them at work ? Now turn the other way." The sound came again, precisely in front. " They are a long way off yet. Can you make out how they are going to strike us, boys ? " Conrath asked of the guard.

" You can't tell for sure, the rock is so deceivin' ; but they seem to be comin' straight for the end of the drift."

" Who are *they ?* Who are coming ? " Cecil demanded.

" The Led-Horses, my dear. They may blast through any day or night, but they 'll find we 've blocked their little game."

" What is their game ? " Mrs. Denny inquired.

" They claim our new strike, and, from the sound, they seem to be coming for it as fast as they can ! "

Cecil locked her arms in the folds of her

long, shrouding cloak, and a nervous shudder
made her tremble from head to foot.

"Poor little girl!" said Conrath, putting
his arm around her shoulders; "I ought to
have taken you straight home after the fright
you got in the drift."

"Why, do you know," said Mrs. Denny,
looking a little pale herself, "I think this is
awfully interesting. I'd no idea that beauteous young Hilgard was such a brigand.
Just fancy, only two nights ago you were
dancing with him, Cecil!"

"What?" said Conrath, turning his sister
roughly toward him with the hand that rested
on her shoulder. She moved away, and stood
before him, looking at him, her straightened
brows accenting the distress in her up-raised
eyes.

"Why should I not dance with him? In
this place you all suspect each other, and
accuse each other of everything. He accuses
you. Shall Mrs. Denny, on that account, refuse
to dance with you?"

She spoke in a very low voice, but Conrath replied quite audibly, "Don't be a fool,
Cecil!"

"Oh," she said, letting her arms fall before her, desperately, "it is *all* the wildest, wildest folly that any one ever heard of! Men, fighting about money — that is n't even their own! Why, this is not mining, it is murder!"

"We 're not fighting," Conrath replied. "Half the mines in the camp are showing their teeth at each other; — it 's the way to prevent fighting. If they keep on their own ground there won't be any trouble; but," turning to Mrs. Denny with a darkening look, "if I catch that 'beauteous' friend of yours on my ground, he 'll be apt to get his beauty spoiled."

On their way back along the drift, they were warned by a spark of light and a distant rumbling that a car was approaching along the tram-road. They stopped, and, lowering their candles, stood close against the sloping wall while the car passed. It was at the entrance to another dark gallery, and as the car rolled on, the warm wind of its passage making their candles flare, it left them face to face with a miner, who had also been overtaken at the junction of the drifts. He was tall, and his face was in deep shadow from the candle fastened in the crown of his hat. He stepped back into the side-drift, pulling his hat-brim down.

"Who was that?" Mrs. Denny asked.

"I didn't notice him," Conrath replied. "One of the Cornish-men on the last shift. I don't know all their faces."

"He doesn't walk like a Cornish-man," said Mrs. Denny, looking after him, "and his hand was the hand of a gentleman." They moved on a few paces in silence. Cecil flagged a little behind the others, and then dropped to the floor of the drift in a dead faint.

It was the air, they said,—and the nervous shock she had suffered while alone in the ore-chamber.

She let them explain it as they would, only begging to be left to recover herself quietly in her own room.

When the little stir of Mrs. Denny's departure had subsided, and the house was once more silent, Cecil rose, still pale, and shuddering with slight, successive chills, and sought the snug warmth of the kitchen. It was early twilight, but a lamp had been lit on the shelf above the ironing-table, where the maid was at work, rubbing and stretching her starched cuffs, and clapping the iron down at intervals on its stand. From time to time she bestowed a glance of sympathy on her young mistress's dejected figure, crouching by the stove, her hands extended toward the steam from the kettle.

"Molly, if anything should happen at the mine, would the engine stop right away?" Cecil asked, after a long silence.

"Why, yes, Miss, if anything broke."

"No, I mean if any one were hurt."

"Well, if 't was one of the men, maybe they would n't stop," said Molly, gravely lifting a fresh iron from the stove, and inverting it close to her glowing cheek. "The pumpin'-engine don't never stop, unless somethin' breaks, or the mine shuts down for good an' all."

"But if it were — if anything should happen to my brother?"

"They 'd stop, if the superintendent was hurt — of course they would, Miss."

"The engine would stop?" Miss Cecil repeated, lifting her head from the supporting hand on which it had rested.

" Yes, Miss, it would."

They were both silent, while Cecil seemed to listen. " Mr. Conrath is not under ground, is he, Miss?"

" No, he went down to the camp with Mrs. Denny; — will you open the door a moment, Molly?"

Molly opened the door and stood against it, folding her bare arms in her apron, — a warm, bright figure, with the gray, cold sky of twilight behind her. The heavy heart-beats of the engine came distinctly from the shaft-house. Cecil went to the door and stood beside Molly, looking out at the dull sky, and the new, unpainted buildings, crudely set in the low-toned landscape of evening.

"Do you hear the other engine?" Cecil asked, after a moment's doubtful listening.

"The one over yon, Miss? I hear it plain — wait now! It comes faint-like, between. Was you thinkin' anythin' would be happenin'?"

" I'm always thinking something will happen," said Cecil, a deep sigh following her long-suspended breath.

" Yes, there's a mort o' trouble with them mines ! 'Most every day some of 'em gets hurt. They gets a bucket dropped on their heads, or a rope breaks, or a blast goes off; or they sets a kag o' that Giant on the stove to warm it, and it goes off on 'em and tears everything to pieces."

" What is ' Giant,' Molly?"

" It's a kind of powder, Miss — awful inno-cent-lookin' stuff, like cold grease — but it do send a lot o' them poor fellows out o' the world ! They gets careless, that's what the companies says."

" Do you know anybody in the mines, Molly ?"

" Why, yes, Miss. My brother's on the Led-Horse, and I know another o' the boys across the gulch."

" Molly ! how strange that is !"

" Is it, Miss ? Sure, I don't know why ! Tom's been over there since ever Mr. West come. He worked under him in Deadwood. He likes Mr. West first-rate, an' he likes Mr. Hilgard."

"Who put Mr. West in, do you know?"

"Mr. Hilgard, Miss. They was a loafin', drinkin' set over there when he come out from the East to take holt, and he could n't make nothin' of 'em ; an' so he clears out the whole lot of 'em, and Gashwiler at the head of 'em and the worst one of all, to put in Mr. West an' a new gang o' men."

"Gashwiler — do you mean *our* captain?"

"I do, Miss!"

"Oh, Molly! I never knew that! Shut the door — I'm so cold! I never knew it!" she repeated, gazing at Molly desolately.

"It might be you did n't, Miss — but it's the truth. Mr. Conrath maybe'd pack me out of the house for sayin' it, but it's my belief that Gashwiler's making the whole trouble between 'em. He knows the Led-Horse, every inch of it, Miss, and where their ore is, just 's I could come in here and lay my hand on the flour-barrel in the dark."

Again in silence they listened to the beat of the engines.

"When do the men on the three-o'clock shift come up, Molly?"

"At eleven o'clock, Miss."

" Why, how long they stay down there ! ".

" Eight hours it is, above ground, and eight below. I bet it seems long to them that 's below ! "

" Oh ! " said Cecil, lifting her hands, and pressing them on the top of her head, " I wish they would *all* resign ! "

VIII.

THE SHOSHONE KITCHEN.

CECIL's life at the mine was a lonely one.
Even the ladies who lived in the populous
parts of the camp struggled vainly to fulfil
duly that important feminine rite, the exchange
of calls. There were difficulties of roads and of
weather, and of finding the missing houses of
acquaintances, which, in the progressive state
of the city topography, had been unexpectedly
shunted off into other streets. A new street
had barely time to be named and numbered,
before it was moved backward or forward,
or obliterated altogether, in the intermittent
attempts of the city government to recon-
cile United States patents with "jumpers'"
claims.

Cecil, two miles from the post-office, at an
isolated mine, was out of the reach of all but
the most persevering efforts of her new friends.
In truth, there were not many of them. Cecil

was a shy girl, just out of school, with a habit
of showing surprise at a great many things
that were taken as a matter of course in the
camp. Hilgard had one consolation in his
exile from all chance of her favor: there was
no one else who could boast of it.

The kitchen and parlor at the Shoshone
were separated from each other only by a
short flight of steps, and a square, dark passage, which opened also into Conrath's office.
Mistress and maid, living so near together,
and being of nearly the same age, did not pretend to a very formal relation. The sounds
from the kitchen plainly described to Cecil,
in the parlor, the nature of Molly's opera-
tions. When they were loud and urgent;
when Molly took the field with her canvas
apron girt round her hips, and her wash-tubs
in solid array; when armfuls of wood thun-
dered into the wood-bin, or crockery rattled, or
resonant tins responded to her vigorous touch,
the young mistress kept within her own precincts; but when footsteps trod peacefully to
and fro between the stove and the ironing-
table, and the clap of the iron sounded at
intervals, or when apples bumped comfort-

ably from the pan on Molly's knees to the one on the floor beside her, Cecil ventured out, with her sewing, or sat idle on the steps, nursing her arms in her lap, and watching Molly's monotonous movements with the pleased, curious content of a child.

These visits had increased somewhat in frequency since Miss Conrath's discovery that the affections of her maid were temporarily deposited in the Led-Horse.

Molly had silently noted this fact, and hinted it to her brother, and to a tall young timber-man who crossed the gulch with him occasionally, and spent an evening in the Shoshone kitchen. The young timber-man had been one of the two men at the cranks, who had hoisted Hilgard to the surface on the morning of his first meeting with Miss Conrath. He recalled this incident for Molly's benefit, who gave it its full value, and beamed over it with the broadest satisfaction.

"Sure I could see a good way out of it," was her hearty if somewhat premature suggestion. "Let them consolidate the mines an' put Mr. Hilgard over 'em both, an' let her choose which side of the gulch she'd live.

I would n't live over there," Molly continued, indicating, with a depreciative toss of her head, the Led-Horse side of the gulch, " for all you 've got in the mine."

" It 's not much, thin ! " Tom interposed, confidentially.

" The water is that hard, it 's enough to take the skin off your hands," Molly continued, " and the ground 's as black as the stove, with the crock off o' thim burnt woods, an' every man o' you leavin' the print of his fut on the floors. Sure I might be on me knees from mornin' to night, and they 'd never look clean ! "

" You 'd not be scrubbin' floors if you was over there ! " the young timberman remarked, with emphasis that brought the color into Molly's cheeks.

" And who 'd be doin' it for me ? " she asked, in a high voice. " Is it the men that scrubs the floor over there and the women that works underground ? "

Cecil, alone in the silent parlor, heard the burst of boyish laughter that followed this sally, and said to herself, rather wistfully, that the Shoshone kitchen was much the most cheerful room in the house.

On the days after these evening visits,
Molly was unusually communicative, and had
a great deal of information to give on the
progress of the dispute between the mines.
Cecil did not always restrain her when she
sometimes inadvertently passed from an attitude of respectful neutrality to one of undisguised enthusiasm for the side of the Led-
Horse. It was best to hear both sides, Cecil
said to herself; but she heard very little on
the side of the Shoshone in these days.

It was becoming more and more difficult to
talk to her brother of his affairs, and to ask
for his confidence. He seemed unusually pre-
occupied. He often came home late at night,
having dined down town, and breakfasted
alone in the long parlor at ten or eleven
o'clock the next morning. Cecil, taking her
walk on the windy porch, would run in for
a moment to pour his coffee, perching opposite him with her hat on, and the wings of
her cloak thrown back from her pretty arms.
She would carry his cup round the table to
him, bestowing the kiss of custom on his
pale, unshaven cheek. He received it generally with fraternal indifference, but some-

times he would pull her down on the broad
arm of his chair, pinch her small chin, and
tell her, with careless hyperbole, that she was
the prettiest girl west of the Mississippi.   And
she would scold him for drinking such very
black coffee in such a large cup.

" Look at your hand, how it shakes, you
stupid boy ! A man never knows how to take
care of his health, and you won't let me take
care of yours for you."

" Take care of your own, Cecy," he would
say. " You were always the best of the whole
lot of us."

Once she reminded him of an old promise to
ride with her every day in the valley, and read
aloud to her in the evenings.

" If we don't begin soon," she complained,
" the valley will be covered with snow.   I
have n't had my habit on for six weeks, and
I 've read everything in the house, through and
through, alone here by myself all day long."

" Poor little Cecy ! it is a dull cage for such
a pretty bird !" Conrath would reply. " Never
mind ; when Shoshone stock is up to thirty,
we 'll have some good horses, and we 'll go
East every winter and have our friends out

here in summer, — and a dinner-party twice
a week. You could go back at any time,
you know, if you're getting tired of it."

"You know I don't want to go back, or
to have dinner-parties, or anything like that.
I only wish you would treat me more —
more as if I could be trusted to know about
things."

"About what things, for instance?"

"About your troubles with the Led-Horse.
Have they blasted through?"

"No, they haven't yet. You've never forgotten that barricade, Cecy. Now you see
how impossible it would be to tell you things,
as you say. The simplest thing would seem to
you quite frightful. Girls ought not to know
what is going on in a place like this. That's
one reason why I am not so much troubled
about your loneliness. It's better for you not
to hear all the gossip of the camp, — it would
make you unhappy."

This was the most intimate conversation
they had had for weeks. A few days afterward, Molly informed her mistress that the
Led-Horse had blasted through on a level
with the Shoshone barricade. Cecil gave a

gasp at this news. Molly, however, assured
her that everything was peaceable. The Led-
Horse had no guard, and no barricade
except the loose rock that had fallen with the
last blast; but its lawyers had gone down to
the session of the district court at D—— with
important testimony, and by this time the
injunction was virtually granted. That was
probably the reason why Conrath had turned
so silent, and was busier than ever, Cecil
thought. She still persisted in the belief
that Gashwiler was responsible, and that her
brother had been deceived up to the point
of a distressing awakening from his costly
delusion.

It was nearly the middle of September.
The season was over, when daily the dry
winds whirled across the porch, shook the
loose sash and, flinging a cloud of yellow dust
against the pane, carried their rude message
from house to house of the little settlement,
and on along the white road to the camp.
The season of rains was over, when daily the
cold showers hurtled on the roof, and blotted
out the valley ; when wild flowers blossomed
on the pass, and lined the cañons, with a

phantasmal beauty. The late, passionless summer had come to the weary, tempestuous year, just as summer elsewhere was taking her leave. Was this a place for men, Cecil murmured to herself in her lonely walks, where even the grass, that commonest vegetable joy, gave up the ghost and withered in the autumn, as sparse and feeble as in the earliest spring!

The day after the news of the injunction, Cecil resolved once more to approach her brother on the subject of his troubles. She lay in the hammock, which was stretched across the long room, her slippered feet to the fire, the light from the low window shining on the top of her cushioned head, listening for the clink of a horse's hoof on the frozen ground. She listened and waited, until sunset faded into twilight and lamps were lit. Dinner was indefinitely postponed, and Cecil took a slight meal and a lonely cup of tea by the fire. With a book in one hand she read, and sipped her tea and listened, alternately. She heard the outer door of the kitchen shut; silence followed — absolute silence all over the house.

It was very strange of Molly to have gone out without permission at that hour, leaving her mistress alone in the house. When the girl came in, fully two hours afterward, Cecil took no notice of her, not venturing to speak while she felt hurt and vexed. Molly, however, was too much excited to remark her mistress's mood. Her hair was disordered, and her cheeks were flushed and shining with wind-dried tears. She came straight to the fire, kneeling on the rug and asking, in a loud whisper, —

"Is Mr. Conrath home yet?"

"You know that he is not," Cecil replied without looking up from her book.

"There's something I must tell you, Miss Cecil, if I was to leave the house to-night!"

"You seem to have done that, already, Molly, without regard to me."

Then, as Molly turned her face away and put her apron to her eyes, Cecil abandoned her attempt at dignity and leaned toward the girl impulsively.

"Why, Molly, what is it?" she said, putting her hands on her shoulders and pulling her toward her. "What are you crying about?"

Molly put down her apron.

"You've a right to know it, Miss," she sobbed, "if it is your own brother; and Tom isn't one to meddle except to save trouble. Mr. Conrath, maybe, would kill me for speakin'. Gashwiler would, anyway!"

"Don't run on so, Molly! Wait a minute and tell me quietly; and don't tell me anything but the truth."

"It's Mrs. Gashwiler, Miss, that it comes from, and I'd believe every word, for she's an honest woman, though as hard as a nail — and what would it be to her interest? She's got the same grudge as her man has against Mr. West and Mr. Hilgard. It's little she'd care, if it wasn't for Tom."

Cecil sat helpless under the confusion of Molly's words, feeling, in her suspense, that they were fraught only with misery.

"Tom was always good to her young ones when he boarded with 'em. He was packin' the little lame one about whenever he got the chance, and she's never forgot it of him. She heard somethin' one night between her man and Mr. Conrath. She was wakin' with the toothache, and the walls is nothin' but lath.

She would n't tell Tom what it was, but she got at him to leave the Led-Horse, for fear he'd get into trouble along with it. And she made him promise he'd never tell on her. And he's kep' it till he says it hangs on him that heavy that he's bound to speak. But it's to you he bid me come with it. He'll not go to one o' his own side, but, says he, ' Mrs. Gash can't complain of me for speaking to Mr. Conrath's own sister ; for she's a Shoshone, and who's got a better right to know what diviltry he's up to?'"

"Mr. Conrath, Molly — my brother?"

"Mr. Conrath's in it, not a doubt o' that ; an' it means trouble to the Led-Horse, or Gash's wife would never be after Tom to try to get him out of it. An' he won't stir for me, Miss ! He'll stick by his own side." Here Molly's sobs broke forth. "For God's sake, Miss Cecil, you'll not go to Mr. Conrath with it!"

"Molly, whom am I to go to?" Cecil's lips were white, and her voice had sunk almost to a whisper.

"Go to Mr. Hilgard, Miss ! Tell him to look out for himself an' for them that's under

him, an' to put more than a heap o' rocks between him an' Gashwiler's barricade. What
good 'll his lawyers do him, when they 've
jumped him. That 's what Tom says, Miss,"
Molly went on, in her loud, vehement whisper. "He says they 're gone, if the law
takes holt ; they 'll have to pay back every
dollar's worth of ore they robbed Mr. Hilgard
of, an' it 'll ruin them," cried the girl, reckless that she was speaking to a Shoshone.
"And they 're waiting for a chance to jump
the mine. 'They 'll clean her out,' says Tom,
'before ever the law 'll give it back.' "

"Molly, do you ask me to go to a stranger
to warn him against my brother ? You must
be crazy. I cannot go to any one but my
brother. I shall tell him nothing that you
have told me. I am not going to betray *your*
brother. I will ask him — oh, I will make him
give it all up, and let us leave this place !"

"He 'll never do it, Miss ! no more than
Tom 'll leave the Led-Horse for me askin'
him."

"Molly, please go away, and let me think
about it by myself. You are a good girl to
come to me ; you can trust me. If I cannot

do any good, I will not do any harm. I must see my brother to-night. If it is no use, then we will think of some other way."

The two girls clung to each other with tears running down their cheeks.

" You'd be speakin' for them all, Miss, if you went to Mr. Hilgard. Sure, whatever hinders a fight is for one the same as another."

" How could it hinder anything if I went to Mr. Hilgard?"

" If he'd stop his lawin' an' put five good men in the drift, wid a barricade in front of 'em, Gash'd never touch him! That's what Tom says."

" Do you suppose, you poor child, that Tom knows better than Mr. Hilgard?"

" He does, Miss, when Mr. Hilgard don't know what I'm after tellin' you!"

It was late that night when Conrath returned. Cecil sprang up quickly, her heart beating hard and fast, when she heard his horse's hoofs on the wooden bridge leading to the stable. From the sounds, Conrath was having some difficulty in forcing his horse over the narrow passage. There were signs of obstinacy and nervousness on the part of the horse, and of temper on that of the rider. As the plunging and backing continued, Cecil became alarmed. She ran to Molly's door and woke her, asking for Peter, the stable-man.

"Why does n't he go to Mr. Conrath?" she demanded. "He can't get Andy over the bridge."

Molly did not know where Peter was, and Cecil, hearing Andy suddenly clatter across the disputed ground and stop at the stable, went back herself, shivering, to the parlor.

Conrath was a long time getting into the house. He climbed up the end of the piazza, apparently with a good deal of trouble, bumping his knees and elbows on the piazza floor, in his progress.

"Why doesn't he come around to the steps?" Cecil wondered. " It must be very dark."

She opened the door; it was not at all dark. The moon had risen, and Conrath's shadow was thrown up against the side of the house, as he came along the piazza, walking with a heavy, careful step. He passed her at the door, neither noticing nor speaking

10

to her, and, crossing the room, sank into a seat by the fire, without removing his hat.

He slouched in his chair, in a helpless, disorganized attitude, moving his eyes vacantly from her face to his own hands, which hung feebly in his lap.

She knelt before him, without touching him. She looked long in her brother's face, studying, with intense, heart-broken scrutiny, the familiar features, over which some mysterious, sickening influence had passed. The change was very slight. Mrs. Denny would have understood it instantly. Many of Conrath's friends would have been amused by it. Gradually the meaning of it came to Conrath's sister, but it did not amuse her. She recoiled from him slowly, rising to her feet, a cold, incredulous disgust whitening her cheeks and her lips. It was too cruel a mockery of her reliance on him. She went away to her room and hid herself from the sight of him, leaving him to sleep off the effects of his "predilection" by the fire.

Cecil did not sleep; she lay in the darkness hour after hour, shuddering, with dry, convulsive sobs. The trouble she had looked

in the face that night she knew was a
wretchedly common one, but she had never
believed that it could touch her own life. She
reproached herself for deserting the shabby
figure in the chair before the fire, but to-night
she could not feel that it was her brother. If
that were her brother, where then could she
look for help?

She made no effort to see Conrath the next
day; in fact, she kept out of the way of see-
ing him until he had left the house. At noon,
she went to Molly with a note and asked her
to see that Mr. Hilgard received it promptly.

" You must give it to him yourself, Molly,
or to Mr. West."

" Thank you, Miss Cecil," said Molly, taking the note.

" It may not do any good," the girl said
wearily, " and I am not doing it for you any
more than for myself."

" Did you sleep any the night, Miss?"

" Why should I sleep? Did you sleep yourself, Molly?"

" I did, Miss; but the heart of me was
wakin' and dreamin.' I dreamt Mr. Conrath
was a draggin' you over the bridge, an' him

on Andy; an' you was pullin' back, but he
had you by the hand an' would n't let go."

"It is easy to see how you came to dream
that, Molly," said Cecil, a slow, painful blush
burning itself upon her cheek. "Do you remember my knocking at your door?"

"Did you, Miss? Last night, was it?"

"Yes, it was last night; and it was Andy,
not I, who would n't go over the bridge. My
brother would not have to drag me, if he
wanted me to follow him anywhere."

Cecil kept by herself all day. She could
not bear even Molly's eyes upon her, while
she was learning to bear the first pressure of
the new and ignominious grief, which she had
put on like a garment of penitence under the
soft robes of her girlhood.

IX.

BETWEEN DAYLIGHT AND DARK.

THE sun was just below the Shoshone hill. The black, denuded pines on the hill-top leaned toward each other, or stood erect against the yellow light that streamed upward and broadened outward, through a thin, gray cloud that overspread the western sky.

Cecil was hurrying down the unused trail, to meet Hilgard at the blazed trees. She felt they would be safe there from interruption. Her heart was too heavy to flutter with girlish doubts and tremors. She sped along, beating back with her rapid footsteps the folds of her sombre cloth dress.

Hilgard was waiting for her, walking about impatiently, one hand in the side pocket of his closely buttoned pea-jacket, the other holding the cigarette he was mechanically smoking. She had kept him waiting three quarters of an hour; he was feeling half angry and cheated, and altogether disappointed, when he saw her coming, among the gray-stemmed aspens, that were dropping all their pale gold leaves in the grasp of the autumn winds. He started toward her at once, forgetting his grievance at the first sight of her face. She explained hurriedly that some ladies from the camp had called and detained her.

"You know it is only trouble that brings me here."

He restrained some passionate exclamation, and said, as humbly and quietly as he could, —

"I knew, of course, it was not for your own pleasure or mine."

"And you must have known it was the old trouble — between the mines," she went on, without heeding his words. "I have thought of a way that might make things less — less unhappy." She hesitated, and he waited for her to explain.

"I have been told that you are likely to get the injunction against my — against the Shoshone; there will be claims for damages against us which may be hard to settle —"

"Against *you* — great Heavens! They are

not my claims, and they are not against your
brother. Can't you make it more impersonal ?"

" I am afraid I cannot," she said, gently ;
" our side has been in the wrong. I believe
that now. It is right that you should
triumph."

" Why will you call it my triumph ? If
you could have the faintest idea what I'm
paying for it !."

" It is your triumph, and you will be as-
sociated with it if you stay to see it finished.
And the failure and disgrace will be asso-
ciated with — my brother. Wait a moment,
please — " She put her hand up to the black
scarf that swathed her throat, as if to still
the " climbing sorrow " there. " I have not
come to apologize for my brother, but — I —
I believe he has been deceived ! He has had
bad counsel. This is the first — first — "
· She could not go on, and Hilgard bowed
his head before her.

" I am sure he has," she began again, in her
voice of stifled misery. " And this person
who I think has betrayed him, is an enemy
of yours. I am sure of that too. He is a

man with an old grudge against you, and
against your mine. No one can tell how
much this may have been with him in his
influence over my brother. He might never
have shown it. Don't you see how it might
embitter a dispute like this, and make it personal, and how much harder it would make
the settlement? The triumph of your side
would be very hard for your enemy to bear.
You would be hated."

"These old grudges are not so dangerous
as you think; men hold them till they get
used to them, and take a certain satisfaction
in them. I think I know the man you speak
of, but there are a great many men in the
camp with grudges against me. One expects
that in a place of this kind."

"You don't see what I mean," she said,
with a despairing sigh. "I want you to remove part of the cause of this trouble, before
the time for the final settlement comes."

"You want me to remove myself?" he
asked.

"Yes, I want you to go away and let some
one else come to do that part. Then it will
be only between the mines."

" You ask me to resign ? "

" Yes, I do," she repeated, with sad persistence.

The words struck to the very core of his weakness. He had himself pondered the joyless situation and counted the cost of its issues. The injunction was certain to be granted, and the suit for damages could but develop either inefficiency on Conrath's part, or a deliberately dishonorable policy. If that policy had been successful, it was not likely that any questions would have been asked at the Shoshone home office; but unsuccessful rascality was not likely to find favor even with Conrath's " company." The triumph of the Led-Horse would be complete. The arrears of its expenses could be paid out of the Shoshone ore-bins. Hilgard's own infatuated tenacity, as it had probably seemed to his president, would be justified, — and then ? He would go on living on his barren hill, with his hidden loss and defeat burdening his spirit. The triumph would still be Conrath's, through his sister. But if now, at this point in the contest, with the cause of the Led-Horse safe in the hands of the law, he might step out and escape the odium of success !

She stood by the blazed pine, pressing her ungloved hands hard against its corrugated trunk, and looking at him with an imploring suspense in her eyes. It was more than youth and passion could bear.

" Cecil," he said, trying to steady his low accents as he spoke her name for the first time, " there is only one reason why I should do this. I have no real enemies except those who keep me from you. If you will ask me to go for your sake, I will go to-night. Do you ask me to go in that way ?"

" Oh, I ask it, — I ask it! What does it matter how I ask it? What does anything matter ? "

" But it matters all the world to me! I am not doing this for fear of any man's hatred, but for love of you. I have no business to go — my place is here until everything is settled. But if a scruple is to cost me my life's happiness, — it is too much to pay. Shall I go for you, my love ?"

" Do I ask you too much ? Is it a sacrifice of your honor ? "

Her eyes still pleaded, although she forced herself to give him a chance for retreat.

BETWEEN DAYLIGHT AND DARK.

"Don't ask me now. I don't know what honor is. I only know what love is. I will go for you."

He took her hands, with the print of the rugged pine-bark on their tender palms, and held them up to his face and laid them about his neck. They clung there a moment. Her heavy hat fell back, and her fair, unsheltered head drooped against the rough folds of his coat.

"If I should go, how will it be when we meet again? I shall not be on the other side, then?"

"No," she murmured.

"You will come to me, whatever side I am on?"

"Yes."

"I have your promise, Cecil?"

"Yes, unless — "

"No, nothing but your promise!"

Her arms slipped down.

"But a great deal may happen before we meet again — "

"Yes, but when, or where, or how we meet, you are mine, dearest, remember!"

"Have I promised that?"

"That, or nothing. Don't play with me, Cecil. Either you mean it, or you do not. I am in dead earnest. There is no reason for my going, except that you ask me, — the girl I love!"

"You must go," she said, pushing him from her. "You are going to-night!"

"To-night! But why to-night?"

"Please, please go! I want you to go to-night. I shall not dare to be happy until you are gone."

"I might go," he said, doubtfully, "if there is time."

"There is plenty of time — you said you would go to-night. When the train goes out, will you be on it, George?"

She let him kiss her hands and draw from her finger a little ring, — a slight, school-girl token; she scarcely knew what he was doing.

"I want something to make it seem true. You have always been such a hopeless dream. Is it true?" he whispered, passionately. "Am I sure of you, darling?"

Not so sure but that, in a moment, she had slipped out of his arms and was running

away in the gathering dusk, that made her
figure almost one with the dun hillside. He
had nothing but her ring clasped in his hand.
He turned away, trembling and half stupefied.
His foot struck one of the low, gray monument stones, and he staggered forward, saving
himself, with a heavy jar, against a tree-trunk.
Recovering from the shock, he missed the
ring. He searched for it long, stooping and
groping about on the rough ground, sifted over
with trodden pine-needles. At last, when
twilight settled darkly in the hollow of the
hills, he gave up his quest and took the homeward path, a pang of bereavement chilling
his new-born bliss.

He went to his office, wrote two or three
letters and telegrams, and from the drawers
and pigeon-holes of his desk he collected a
number of papers and note-books, which he
placed in a heap on the lid. He then went
deliberately around the room, picking up
various articles, in preparation for his pack-
ing. With all these in one arm, he was about
to put out the lamp, when he saw a sealed
telegram lying on the floor behind his desk.
It might have been blown off when he opened

the door. It was with a strange reluctance
he put down his burden and opened the telegram. The spirit of the change was upon
him. He was impatient to be gone. At
D—— he would see his lawyers and leave
with them certain directions and papers for
the forthcoming trial, write his farewells to his
few friends in the camp from there, and start
eastward at once. His formal resignation lay
on the desk, directed to his president.

The telegram was from Wilkinson. It read:
" Thrown out of court by technicality. Look
out for jumpers."

He read the message over two or three times,
then folded it and placed it in a note-book
which he took from the breast of his coat.
He did not take up his armful of properties
again, but sat down by the desk, looking
fixedly at the sealed letters before him. If
temptation had been strong with him in the
gulch, it was stronger now that he had yielded
the first step ; and if his happiness had seemed
at stake before, there were possibilities in this
new situation which made his heart stand still.

" No, by heaven ! " he exclaimed, pushing
back his chair. " I 've gone far enough. Let

them get some one else to do police duty for them ! "

Nevertheless, he took up his letter to the president and tossed it into the fire. The other letters and telegrams followed. This was no time for resignations. He would see West at once.

On inquiry, West was not to be seen. He had gone down to the camp. Hilgard went to his room, pulled open his bureau drawers, and began shoving various articles hastily into a travelling-bag. He sat on the side of his bed, with the bag between his knees. When it was packed, he still sat motionless in the same position, rigid with the silent struggle that possessed him.

A knock came at the door of the outer room. It was unlighted, except by the broad glow of the fire. Hilgard opened to West, just returned from the camp.

" Come in, West, I want to see you."

" I want to see *you*, sir."

While Hilgard hunted for Wilkinson's telegram in his pocket-book, West produced a scrap of gray hardware paper, and held it out to his chief.

" Just look at that, sir. I picked it up to-night on the counter at Bolton & Trivet's."

Hilgard stooped, and held the paper to the fire-light, while West, turning round, with his lean, chilled brown hands behind him, spread their palms to the warmth.

The paper bore a memorandum made with a broad, soft pencil.

800 *Car.*

50 *Win.*

Shoshone.

Hilgard produced his telegram and handed it with the paper to West.

" There you are," he said.

" Yes, sir.   There's the whole infernal business," West replied, as he studied the telegram.   " It shows what they think of us," he added, with a grim smile.   " They dassent try it on with less than fifty Winchesters."

" You can't make anything else out of it, West ? "

" There ain't anything else to make.   It's an old game ! I 've more 'n half expected it. I looked round a little, while I was down 'to

the camp," he continued, in his slow, quiet
drawl, " and got track o' some boys that I
can depend on. Told 'em they 'd better come
along up soon 's they could. They 'll come
all fixed. If you don't like it, sir, it won't
make a bit o' difference to them. They can
keep their mouths shut."

" It 's all right — it 's the only way."

Hilgard stepped back and closed the bedroom door on his preparations for departure.
West stood with his back to the fire, his eyes
fixed on the toe of his extended boot, which
he grated back and forth on the bricks of the
hearth. He did not lift his eyes as Hilgard
came toward him again, but remarked to the
toe of his boot, —

"Wish *you 'd* git out of the camp. To-night
ain't any too soon. You can trust the Old
Horse to me, sir ! I 'll hold her in spite of
hell !" He looked up now, with a keen gleam
lighting his blue eyes. " Damn it, *you 've* got
friends in the East ! "

" I have one friend here, it seems," said
Hilgard.

The two men looked into each other's faces,
silently.

" We 'll hold her together, West!— Come, there 's no time to talk ! "

At twelve o'clock that night, West and Hilgard were hurrying over the frozen ground toward the shaft-house. The old moon had risen with a circle round her imperfect disk. Long, white clouds were banked in the southern sky, and there was a chill foreboding of snow in the air.

" She has n't shut down," West remarked, looking across the gulch toward the Shoshone.

" Very likely she won't; it 's a good blind for us, and she has men enough. They must have noticed that we are all quiet over here."

" I took care of that, sir. I told Tom Ryan to give out, kind o' promisc'us, down to the boardin'-house, that we 're in a kind of a scrape over here — pump broke down. He 's always jawin' back and forth with 'em."

" West, I wish you had n't done that," Hilgard said, sharply.

West replied with some heat, —

" Good Lord ! They 're five to one — ain't

that enough ? If they want to try it on, let 'em try it to-night ! "

There was an ominous stillness in the Led-Horse shaft-house. The low moon looked in through the bare, dusty windows, where a group of men with rifles slanted between their knees sat around an old cast-iron stove. The engine was silent. The only sounds in the dim place were the steady boring of an auger in the hands of some person unseen, and the fire, leaping and roaring in the stove, which had flushed a sullen red, and emitted sharp lines of light through its cracks. The auger stopped boring as Hilgard and West entered. There was a shoving of gun-stocks and of heavy boots on the gritty floor, but no one spoke.

Hilgard looked about him at the hasty preparations for defence. The iron plates of the platforms had been taken up and turned on edge against the thin board walls. Loaded ore-cars, taken from the tracks, barricaded the weakest points. The auger had been boring loop-holes in the sides of the shaft-house, above the line of protection.

" We 've got you pretty well fixed, up here, boys, if they should make a rush on top."

" They'll be fools to try it," West remarked aside. " You can't shove a lot of ten-dollar fighters against an armed shaft-house ! "

" West, send those six men down the ladders. We'll take the bucket," the superintendent ordered.

" I reckoned I could hold the drift alone, with a Winchester," West ventured, in his most indifferent voice. " A Winchester's mighty comprehensive ! "

Hilgard's eye was on him, but he carefully avoided it. There was an imperceptible stir of appreciation among the men around the stove.

" Two Winchesters will be more comprehensive than one. The fight will be there ! "

" I wish you wouldn't go down, sir," said West, almost shyly.

" That's enough about that, West." Hilgard turned to the men. " Murtagh, take care of the boys up here. Lower us away ! "

At the word, Hilgard and West each grasped the rope and stepped, with a quick, concerted movement, to the edge of the bucket; standing so, face to face, firmly balanced, with rifle in one hand and the shuddering rope in the other, the two men dropped out of sight into the black hole. The rope swung in wider circles; it slapped two or three times against the sides of the shaft; the click of the brake sounded.

"They're down," some one said.

The droning auger began boring again. One of the men by the stove drew his gun across his knees, looked critically at the barrel, wiped it with his sleeve, and said, —

"Hope they won't come up in the bucket with a coat over 'em."

X.

CONRATH COMES HOME.

A YOUNG girl's mood seldom keeps the balance between joy and pain; it will lean, with all the emotional force of her crescent life, alternately to one extreme or the other. Cecil's brief calendar of years had counted no vigil like that of the night before; it was but natural there should be a strong recoil from such intolerable pain. She did not feel the reaction until long after her tryst with Hilgard was over. Her timid joy in that contract was not quick to assert itself. It grew with solemn gladness in the quiet hours, and met with its warm, strong current, the bitter waters that had spread in the watches of the night, laying waste her pride of life. Her pride was prostrate still, but love can do much to heal the wounds of youthful pride.

Cecil walked, with noiseless step, back and forth the length of the fire-lit room; her shadow, mounting the low walls to the ceiling, followed her with grotesque exaggerations of her movements. She was alone, but to-night she felt no loneliness. Since she had first seen him she had never permitted herself to think of Hilgard. But now her eyes drooped, and blushes burned on her cheeks, rebuking the vision that answered her thoughts too vividly. Something in his image, as it came before her that night, troubled her. Was it his beauty, that seemed fit rather for a pageant of love than for love's unseen abnegations? Was it the contrast between Hilgard's knightly integrity and her brother's shabby part in life? She had clothed herself in Conrath's weakness and humiliation, as in a robe of mourning. Would her lover accept her in her weeds? Could her future include both Hilgard and her brother?

The struggle was over in which she had tried to preserve her loyalty to Conrath's cause in the face of a growing conviction that he was in the wrong. She found a certain rest in admitting the truth and falling back on the next lower level of womanly faith, that he had been deceived to the last. Now there would be no more talk of mine and thine. Conrath would go East; he could not desire to stay when this wretched business was over. There, among safer conditions, with old friends around him, he would regain his old life. She could find merciful excuses for him in the past. They had been two motherless children, constantly changed about from one temporary home to another, and from one boarding-school to another, until school days were over. She had known but little of her brother's life in the interval between his school days and the marriage of their father, which had made the brother and sister more dependent on each other. That marriage had not given them a mother; it had only separated them a little more from their father. It was then Conrath had made himself his sister's protector and provider. How proud she had been of his new honors and responsibilities, and how grateful for the home he had brought her to! She stopped, in that terror of the future and its incompatibility with the past, which chilled her dreams of happiness. How could they ever be reconciled?

At bedtime Peter came in with an armful

of heavy green logs for the fire. Cecil went into the kitchen and said good-night to Molly, who was dozing over a novel by the stove; she fastened the doors, wound the clock, and curled herself into the hammock, wrapped in a Navajo blanket. She left the curtains undrawn, — a custom in the camp, that the house might not be dark to a friend outside. She would watch these last hours, until the train went out, and bid her lover a silent, prayerful good-speed.

She swung herself gently to and fro, watching the shadows in the room, chased by the flame-flashes. The hammock swung slower and slower. One arm dropped over its side; the warm, relaxed hand softly unclosed; the long shadow wavering on the carpet rested, and Cecil slept.

The fire flamed and crackled and smouldered down. The sky thickened, and the stars struggled to keep their lookout above the restless lights of the camp. The windows of peaceful, frugal homes were dark, but lights burned still in the house of sickness, in the house of revelry, and in the house of death. Underground, where day and night are inter-

changeable, the ceaseless labor went on.   The
night traffic of the camp went on; late footsteps sounded on the resonant board sidewalks.   Watchers by lonely prospect-holes
renewed their fires.

The moon rose above the hill across the
gulch, and looked in through the window, —
a sinister old moon, leaning with one cheek
awry above a ragged pillow of cloud.   She
knew the strifes and the secrets of the camp.
She looked in many uncurtained windows
that night, upon many sleepers and many
who longed for sleep, and upon many to
whom such fair, innocent sleep as Cecil's
would never come again.   The young girl lay
alone in the shadowy room and slept, while
the night waned, unconscious of the drear procession of to-morrows that awaited the cold,
beckoning finger of daylight.   She slept, while
across the gulch, in another shadowy room,
the defenders of the Led-Horse sat, with
their rifles across their knees, in a fateful
silence.

A log parted, and fell, and rolled forward
on the hearth, filling the room with smoke.
Cecil woke and rose up to mend the fire,

opening the door to let the smoke escape. She stood a moment looking out. It came to her with a shudder, how in that same low light the night before she had waited at the door for her brother's heavy step, and she prayed that he might not come home that way to-night.

At that moment, the eastward-bound train went clanging and rumbling out of the town; its roar was deadened now in the deep cut, now loud again below the hill, dying gradually on the long grades of the first descent. He was gone. Thank God for that! But what was this unwonted stillness of the night? What sound did she miss from those familiar daily and nightly sounds she had ceased to listen for in their continuousness? She listened now, and her own pulses throbbed, heavy and fast, as it came to her that the pulse of the Shoshone had stopped beating. Its engine was silent, and from the opposite hill there came not a sound. Both mines were dumb.

Cecil's first impulse was to waken Molly and send her to the shaft-house for news, but she forbore. " Let her sleep, poor girl," she thought, "it may mean trouble for her as well as for me."

She shrank from going out herself to meet whatever event might be coming. She waited an hour, — an hour of hopeless expectation.

It was now three o'clock. The night had changed; fleecy moving clouds pervaded the sky, and the moon, wading through them as through drifted snow, occasionally showed a bright segment of her disk.

She heard footsteps approaching the house, treading slowly over the frozen mud. They paused near the end of the piazza, and low voices of men spoke together. Then a single tread went quickly around the house to the outer door of the kitchen.

Cecil rose up, wan as a star at daybreak. The first knock came, — low, repeated with brief pauses, as if the knocker listened for some stir within the house.

The footsteps outside moved forward toward the steps of the porch, — a horrible, four-footed human tread, — shuffling nearer, heavily mounting the steps, grating across the floor of the porch, — pausing at the door. Something was laid down at the very threshold of that door.

She could not go and open it.

The knocking continued. A man's step passed along the porch and a face looked in at the window, — looked in Cecil's face and started back.

Slowly she dragged herself the length of the long room and felt her way through the dark passage to the kitchen.

The knocking was loud on the outer door. She crept to the door of Molly's room and heard the girl moving, and her low voice speaking from the window to one outside.

" Whist, for God's sake! I 'm comin' ! "

She clung helplessly to the door, and Molly, opening it, took her in, and half carried her to the bed. She pressed her down into it, and covered her deep under the bedclothes.

" Lie still! Don't stir till I come," she whispered, with her warm cheek laid upon Cecil's.

" Molly, the engines have stopped! I must go myself! It is for me! " Cecil tried to rise in the bed.

" Whatever it is you 'll know soon enough! I 'll come to you with it, Miss Cecil, dear."

Molly shut the bedroom door behind her,

opened the door of the kitchen, and spoke with some one outside. Cecil heard her close the door again, and heard the footsteps outside returning around the house to the porch. Molly went on through the kitchen, carefully closing all the doors behind her, as if the sounds in the house were a pestilent wind from which she would protect her mistress.

Cecil, lying alone in the dark room, benumbed by the keenness of her anguished dread, fell off into a half-unconscious dream of some hovering horror. Suddenly she sprang up. Molly was bending over her. A candle on a stand showed the girl's face plainly. Cecil asked no questions. She rose from the bed, and, holding Molly's hand, followed her in silence back through kitchen and passage to the parlor.

Three miners stood with their backs to the fire. They took off their hats as the women entered, and one of them, a smooth-cheeked young fellow, meeting Cecil's eyes, turned away his own, and rubbed one arm hastily across his face.

That which she had dreaded to see was not there, but one end of the hammock had been unslung; it lay coiled on the floor, and across the place where she had been sleeping, footsteps, crowding upon each other, had printed themselves on the carpet in the yellow mud of the mine, making a diagonal track from the outer door to the door of her brother's bed-chamber.

Cecil's eyes followed that track; then she lifted them to Molly's face, drawing her breath with a deep, hard gasp.

The faithful girl took her young mistress into her arms and gathered her close, rocking her gently in her strong embrace, and moaning over her like a mother over a child in pain that cannot be relieved.

Gashwiler stepped out from the group of three by the fire, saying in the heavy whisper of a man who has no low tones in his voice, —

"Miss, he was dead at the first shot!"

Molly felt a sharp quiver pass over the form locked close in her arms; she darted a fierce glance at Gashwiler, but he went on in his merciless whisper, —

"It was all over, Miss, two hours ago. We lost the fight when he was shot!"

"God help them that begun it!" said Molly, her eyes fixed on Gashwiler's face.

Cecil lifted her head.

"Hush! hush! Let me go to him!"

Cecil looked out the next day on a white world. Snow lay deep on the pass; its soft mantle covered the rugged cañons; it whitened the windward side of the pine-trunks and the gray canvas covers of the freight-wagons, bemired in the deeply rutted roads; it lay smooth on the roofs of the town, and deadened the tramping of feet on the board sidewalks; it had obliterated all the devious footprints of the night before, — it had hidden that track from the Shoshone shaft-house to Conrath's door.

Conrath's door no longer. He would go out of it once more, and then the account between the Led-Horse and the Shoshone would be settled. There was no more talk of mine and thine for Conrath, lying straightened on his unused bed. It had come to Cecil in her long watch beside him that this was the only way in which his future could be reconciled to his past. It was better for him to lie so, his rash struggle over, empty-handed, claiming nothing, refuting nothing. Better that silence, that dignity of rest, that look of his boyhood stealing back over the hardened features of his manhood, than a triumphant bringing home of sheaves that had been wrested from a fellow-laborer. He had atoned to the uttermost, with all that a man has to give in restitution for wrong, — a wrong attempted but not accomplished. The account weighed now on the other side. She was humbly thankful that she would never have to know whose hand had turned the scale.

These were the thoughts that sank, cold and still as the snow-flakes falling from the gray sky, into Cecil's bruised heart, smothering the passion of her grief.

The snow fell all day. It clung to the window-sashes, and melted from the logs that were laid upon the fire. The trail that led down into the gulch was buried out of sight. The yellow gold of the aspens would not be seen again until it had been transmuted into sodden leaf-mould. The low monument-stones were hidden; the scars on the young trees,

12

bearing the marks of human possession, had
been sealed out of sight by the impartial
hand which keeps no record of the contracts
of men; and Cecil's little ring, with its graven
motto, *Dieu vous garde*, lay deep under the
snow.

A few people came from the town that day
of storm to offer their help and sympathy to
the lonely household. Molly received them
all, and spared her mistress the questions and
the exclamations.

Toward dusk Hilgard came ploughing
through the snow to the kitchen door, and
asked Molly if he could see her mistress. A
fire had been kindled in Conrath's office, and
Cecil had spent many hours of the day sitting
there alone. Molly told Hilgard to go into
the parlor, and went herself to the office to
seek her mistress.

Hilgard went into the parlor and found
Cecil there.

Among the rumors of the day that had
come dimly to her ears was one that the
train eastward bound had been blocked by
snow in the valley. When she saw Hilgard
enter the room, she accepted the fact of his

sudden return as the natural result of her longing for him. She had thought he would hear of her sorrow first when he was. thousands of miles away; but the merciful snow had checked him, and the news had brought him back. Bad news travelled quickly, and he would lose no time in coming to her. This was the rapid, unreasoning instinct that took the place of surprise at the sight of him.

She went to him, and all her simple, unquestioning need of him spoke in her face as she raised it to his, putting up her arms like a child.

In the full knowledge of what was before him, he took her in his arms and held her close, in a silent, remorseful embrace.

Drawing his head down to hers, with her hands clasped behind his neck, she whispered, —

"You are all that I have left."

He did not speak, but gently unclasped her hands and moved a little away from her. Would she ever come to him again and put up her arms to him, owning him as her only earthly refuge?

She did not seem to understand his withdrawing from her. She stood a moment looking at him helplessly, and then sat down in the nearest chair.

"Did you hear of it, and come back? You knew how I would need you."

"No, I did not come back."

She kept her eyes on his face, without listening to his words.

"You must not look so! You must not suffer so for me! Ah, think how much worse it might have been! If you had not gone—"

"Cecil, I did not go! You must try not to be hard on me. It had come to the clinch — I could not go!"

"You *must* have gone!" she said, rising and confronting him with her white face of dread. "I heard the train go out."

"I was not on it. Will you sit still, Cecil? I will tell you all."

"I do not wish to hear it — I cannot hear it!"

"Do you think I need not tell you? You will let it rest? God bless you, my dearest!"

"No, no!" she moaned. "You will have to tell me!"

He waited until he could speak, and then spoke fast, in hard, unmodulated sentences.

" I went down to hold the drift. We heard them open the door of the barricade, but we could not see their faces. It was dark in the drift. We called to them to stop. There was firing. I don't know who fired first."

" How many were you ? "

" We were two ! "

" No, no ! " she pleaded, wildly. " There *must* have been more than *two !* "

" The others were not down. Before God, I don't know who did it; it lies between West and me ! "

They looked at each other in the desolate silence that followed, and then she asked, —

" Why did *you* go down ? "

" West would have gone alone. You cannot ask me why I did not let one of my men take my place ? "

" It does not matter," she said.

" No, it does not matter; the responsibility is mine. Cecil, I am the same man you gave your promise to last night. I do not love such work. I went into it, sick at heart. I wish, God knows, I were in his place ! "

"I wish we both were. Oh! my heart is broken!"

"But you cannot mean that it's all over between us? Does it make no difference that it was forced upon me? I have to say it: We were on our own ground; their barricade was fifty feet within our lines. A barricade that is only for defence does not have a door in it; and, Cecil, they were five to one!"

"You are talking about my brother!"

He could say no more.

"I am not judging you," she pleaded, in answer to his look of dumb, passionate despair.

"No, you are only sentencing me without judgment. At least, you will not refuse what poor help I can offer you now? There are things to be done for you which only a man can do. Is there any one here who has a better right than I — than I had last night?"

"They have telegraphed for my father. Oh, forgive me!" she murmured, leaning towards him with an agony of pity in her eyes.

He did not see it. He sat facing the window, and the pitiless, white stare of the snow-laden sky outside. When he spoke again, his voice had lost the accent of appeal.

"I did not know you had a father."

"What have we known of each other? We are strangers. Oh, it has all been too sudden, too rash! It began wrong!"

"Then let us begin over again! I will go away now. I will wait. I will not ask to see you for a long time. But you will give me some hope in the future? I have had no chance to show my love for you. It is true, we do not know each other. But shall we not know each other some day? It is not just to set this awful fatality forever between us!"

She looked at him as if asking him to understand without words, which came so hard.

"I am doing nothing," she said. "It is done already. We must keep apart, because that is the only way to bear it."

"Cecil, you cannot mean it! Why, great Heaven! if I were the lowest criminal, there would be some poor fool of a woman to cling to me! You disgrace me for life. I have done what was simply my duty. But I did n't expect you to feel that. I counted on your mercy. I thought you would forgive me, — as you forgive your brother, — as I forgive him. For, if this is what you mean, Heaven knows, I too have something to forgive!"

"There can be no forgiveness between us," she said, piteously. "Oh, cannot you understand? If you were old or crippled; if your life were spoiled in some way, I would share it with you. I would go away with you now, if I could suffer with you. But, if we were together, we should not suffer. We should be happy — after a while."

"Ah, yes!" he moaned, "we should be happy. What have we done that we should not be happy?"

"You will be happy, I hope — but not with me. Not with — his sister!"

"Why don't you say it out? Am I his murderer, that you hold off from me like that?" Her meek but inflexible resistance maddened him. "Cecil, my little girl, you did love me. Do you love me now? And will you not let me try to heal the hurt I have given you?"

"I love you," she said, resisting his embrace, "but not in that way!"

" There is no other way ! "

" Is there not ? If it hàd been you, instead of him — "

" If it had," — he wrested the words from her, — " and if he were in my place, now, would you disown him for my sake ? "

" I could not do that; I could not break a tie that is in my blood."

" Is there no tie, then, between us ? "

She leaned her head low between her hands.

" We made it ourselves. I made it, selfishly. I made you come to me; do you remember ? "

Did he remember! Only last night her head had rested on his breast; now there was no help or shelter of his she would ever seek again.

She sat with her hands tightly locked together in her lap, white, trembling, but immovable.

" There *is* another way ! If you were — as he is now — would I not love you? You are the same to me as he is; you are dead to me ! "

Her strength suddenly deserted her, and

she broke into wild sobs. He knelt beside her and forced her gently into his arms.

"Cecil, you cannot put me out of your life, like this, with a word! You cannot mean to mock me with a love that denies our very humanity. It is nonsense to say I am dead to you, when every nerve in my body starts at your touch. Did *we* make that tie? It is the oldest, the strongest tie between man and woman. There is no duty that can break it. I am your duty and you are mine, in the sight of God. There is no law that forbids me to love you."

"There is an instinct that forbids *me*,—I must follow that!"

She struggled to her feet. He rose, too, and stood before her, white with the passion of his last appeal.

"You have done your duty, in spite of the cost," she said. "But you cannot judge for me. A woman's duty is different."

A belief that he must, in the end, prevail, had unconsciously supported him, and fed his persistence; but it forsook him now as he looked in her face. He continued to look at her a moment; something like a shiver passed over him; then his words came heavily, like the first sluggish drops following a deep wound.

" Are you so sure that this is your duty ? "

"Oh, if you only had not been so sure of yours!" she faltered, dealing this last blow helplessly, and hearing herself speak as if her voice were the voice of some one else, pronouncing his doom and her own.

There was a loud knock on the outer door. The same ominous hand delivered it that had knocked in the watches of the night before. Cecil started at the sound, and turned, in her terror, to Hilgard. It was the one moment when she might have yielded.

The knock was repeated. She made a gesture toward the door, and as Hilgard turned to open it she escaped from the room.

It was Gashwiler who stood on the threshold.

" Go to the other door!" Hilgard said, fierce with the anguish that was mounting in his blood.

His words were like a curse. The two men looked each other in the eyes for an instant, then Gashwiler retreated down the steps, and around the corner of the house to the kitchen.

Hilgard plunged through the melting drifts that hid the trail, dashing the wet snow from the low fir-boughs. A storm of revolt was let loose within him. He saw no justice, no logic, in his fate. Its mockery was yet in store for him.

XI.

THE HONORS OF THE CAMP.

A TELEGRAM to the home-office, convey-
ing the news of the fight and its result, was
immediately followed by Hilgard's formal
resignation.

This step was not taken from any consciousness of mistaken or excessive zeal, but
from the personal aspect of the situation.
His letter of resignation was accompanied
by a brief statement of the circumstances
that had led to the fight, and which had
made it, so far as the Led-Horse was concerned, inevitable. The answer to his telegram prepared him for the prompt acceptance
of his resignation. It was carefully worded,
and evidently intended as an official comment
on his action. It was as follows : —

" Officers of company deplore unhappy
tragedy of twenty-second. They repudiate

measures requiring sacrifice of life for property.   Less violent policy would better repre-
sent company."

The administration in the East, while con-
ceding discretionary power to the executive
in the West, was keenly sensitive to any
responsibility which might attach to itself
through the exercise of that power.

" They don't repudiate the mine," Hilgard
said to himself, bitterly.   " Their scruples
won't prevent their pocketing the dividends
after they have washed their hands of the
men who saved their property."

For himself he did not care ; it seemed but
a grimace of that fate which had first dealt
him its cruelest blow ; but it hurt him to
think of West.   The only elaborate part of
his letter had referred to West's share in the
discovery and the quenching of the plot.   He
had taken a chief's pride in the loyalty and
courage of his adjutant, and he commended
him earnestly to his successor.   Perhaps
some recognition of his service, the kind of
service that has no price, would come later.
In the mean time he suppressed the telegram.
He was ashamed to read it to the man who

had said, "I reckon I could hold the drift
alone!"

" They think it's a kind of Border-ruffian-
ism," Hilgard said to himself; "they don't
consider it legitimate mining."

It could not add to his hopelessness, but
it embittered it somewhat, to find himself
classed with the very men whose principles he
had sacrificed his life's happiness to defeat.

That element of the camp of which the
Shoshone policy was the exponent accepted
Conrath as its martyr. Gashwiler would
have been a far less interesting figure in
death. He and Conrath were both jumpers;
but Gashwiler was known to be a professional
jumper, while Conrath could claim the dis-
tinction of an amateur. Gashwiler was not
young and handsome, not supposed to come
of a good Eastern family. Gashwiler's family
was a subject of general indifference. He
was not particularly free with his money.
There were no ladies of fashion in the camp
who would be likely to exchange reminiscen-
ces of his attentions to themselves, or com-
pare their respective degrees of intimacy
with the hero of the hour. Even the sober,

thoughtful citizens, who would have dismissed
Gashwiler's removal with the unperplexed
sentiment that he had got his deserts, found
a certain pathos in the fate of his young
chief, cut off by an act of wild justice, at the
beginning of his career.

Few stopped to think what that career was
likely to have been. The more picturesque
portion of the population of the camp was
ready to say, " Poor fellow!" in the general
consciousness that the compassionate epithet
might eventually apply nearer home. Of such
frail clay were they themselves fashioned.

A delay, inexplicable to Conrath's friends,
in the reply to their telegram to his father,
roused a good deal of feeling among them.
It was hastily assumed that Conrath's family
had " gone back " on him. The facts of the
case were, that when the telegram reached
New York, his father was on shipboard between that city and Havana, where his wife
had been ordered by her physician to spend
the winter. The silence was certainly far
from paternal. The camp was sensitive on
the point of its relations with the East, especially in the event of death. Whatever

their indifference or faithlessness to their
Eastern ties during life, the men of Conrath's rank on the frontier confidently expected those ties to contract in the extreme
moment, and restore them to their early
associations.

Without waiting for the silence of Conrath's
father to be explained, the Shoshone partisans
rose in wrathful championship of their in-
sulted comrade, and said : —

"If *they* can't bury him decently, damn
him, we'll bury him ourselves!" The case
of the living sister could wait on that of the
dead brother.

It was on this honorable errand Gashwiler
had come, when he encountered Hilgard in
the first strong agony of his bereavement.

Gashwiler did not see Miss Conrath, but
he had a long and exciting argument with
Molly, who protested that her mistress should
not be disturbed on this or any other business.
She indignantly repudiated, in her mistress's
name, the offered honors to the dead.

"Would n't ye leave her even the body?
Sure, *she'll* never sit behind that hearse —
trailin' through the streets along with the

13

lot of you, an' your music, an' your mil't'ry !
She 's not proud of his dyin', that she 'd want
the whole camp to be throopin' after 'im. ˙ The
least ye can do is to leave him to her now ! ' "

But Molly could not prevail alone against
the resolute sympathy of Conrath's constitu-
ency. All she could do was to soften the
proposition by a little merciful deception, and
present it as a decent, kindly offer to give the
chief of the Shoshone appropriate burial at
the hands of his fellow-Masons and comrades
of the militia regiment to which he had belonged. Cecil gave her helpless consent, with
the condition that all the expenses should be
referred to her father. She was too far pros-
trated in body, as well as in spirit, to know
more of the last scene in the tragedy of her
life, than such dreary echoes as penetrated
the darkened seclusion of her chamber.

Conrath's body was borne out of the house
and conveyed to the camp, where it lay in
state in the unfinished hall of the new Masonic temple, to be gazed upon by the multitude. It was subsequently enshrined in a
plumed hearse, drawn by eight horses, fed
on hay at one hundred dollars a ton. It was

preceded by the regiment of militia, keeping
step through the miry snow of the street,
with guns reversed, to the measures of the
Dead March. The band which furnished
the music was attached to one of the principal variety theatres, and, in the intervals
of its regular performance, was often required to assist at funerals, when the camp
publicly honored some favorite actor in its
social dramas, on his exit from the stage.
The Masonic society marched behind the
hearse in full regalia, followed by the fire
companies and the populace. The latter had
turned out promiscuously, on foot, or mounted
on " livery horses " of uncertain gait and temper, and might be relied on to appear at any
point in the procession, according to its ca-
price, joining the ranks of the Masons, the
militia, or the firemen, and keeping up a
current flow of conversation on topics more
or less relevant to the occasion. The cortége
moved on slowly along the principal streets
of the town, and out through its straggling
suburbs to the cemetery.

The ladies who joined in this public tribute
were easily accommodated in three or four

carriages. In the first of these sat Mrs.
Denny. A prevalent theory of Conrath's
death was that there had been bad blood
between the two young superintendents from
other than business causes; and Mrs. Denny
enjoyed a temporary supremacy among the
ladies of Conrath's preference as the heroine
of this rumor. Hilgard's fate relented toward
him in this one instance, and spared him
the knowledge of this romantic fiction of
the camp, which joined his name with Mrs.
Denny's.

The cemetery was a grim, untended spot,
an acre of the primitive fir-forest, sloping
westward toward the valley, and exposed to
the winds that blew across from the snow-
covered peaks. The fire and the axe had
passed over it, and the nakedness of the land
was left as the inheritance of that peaceful
community which had pitched its low tents
on the bleak slope. A few stumps and stark,
blackened pine trunks, a few young, slight
trees, the sole mourners of the forest, supple-
mented the scant memorials raised to the
human dead. Unpainted boards marked alike
the graves of those who awaited at the hands

of distant friends, removal to a more permanent resting-place, the graves of the poor and
the unknown, and the graves of those, the
place of whose rest was of less importance
to the general public than its finality. The
camp grave-yard, like the camp itself, was
peripatetic. The city was at that time re-
serving the money it might have spent on
its adornment, in contemplation of its removal to another spot.

The heavy, soft snow had sunk and melted
under the high glare of the sun, and lay in
patches, like linen spread to bleach; offering
a grotesque, irreverent suggestion that the
dwellers in those sunken mounds might have
risen in the night and washed their earth-
stained cerements in readiness for the pend-
ing order to "move camp." The funeral
procession, invading this desolate enclosure,
took nothing from its haggard loneliness. It
was impossible to associate the place with
human love and reverence, or even with
humanity's last, enduring rest.

Conrath's body was lowered into the alien
soil. His final allotment of it was small, and
was grudged by none. Here no locator en-

croached upon his neighbor's claim, and the original boundary lines were kept inviolate. A brief stillness fell upon the multitude, diverse and disunited as the stones of a river bed, except in the wave of sentiment which had brought them there; and then the words were spoken, of a common humility and a common hope.

The militia company, drawn up by the side of the grave, fired a volley over it. The second volley scattered badly, and the crowd, recovering from its momentary reflectiveness, echoed the failure with jeers of derision. The mounted mourners had become exalted, during the ceremonies, to a pitch of solemn enthusiasm which could only vent itself in the racing of their horses back to the camp; and the militia company reported at its captain's headquarters before nightfall, and drank to Conrath's repose, in a keg of whiskey opened for the purpose.

Hilgard had considered the spectacle of his victim's last honors, from the sidewalk of the principal street. The moving crowd, keeping pace with the procession, shoved against him, and occasionally pointed at him as an object of interest only second to that concealed from public view in the flag-draped coffin.

That night was Hilgard's last in the camp. At two o'clock of the chill, wan morning, in company with Godfrey, he was on his way to the new railroad station, which had lately superseded the stage office. The empty streets were covered with a light, pure renewal of the previous snows.

" What a ghastly hour for a train to leave ! " the Doctor said, as they walked shiveringly the length of the platform, printing their progress on the untrodden snow. "We're recording ourselves at a great rate on these sands of time. Time here is eternity in the rest of the world. The shipwrecked brother will have to hurry up if he wants to profit by our footprints."

A truck passed them, with Hilgard's trunk piled among the others, eastward bound.

" You 'll take all that 's left of my youth with you, my boy."

" No, Doctor ; you are younger than I am now."

Godfrey stopped and looked earnestly at Hilgard.

"You're morbid, George. You're taking a bigger load on your shoulders than belongs to you. Try to look at it simply, and remember that poor Con did n't know how to live, anyway. He carried too much wick for his candle; he never could have stood a draught. Fate has been kinder to him than to you."

"Doctor, I cannot talk about it!"

"Well, you'd better. It's better to handle a trouble pretty freely, and secularize it, so to speak, before it masters your common sense. I suspect you're hiding a deeper hurt — I won't touch it, boy; only just let me say: Don't think that everything ends here. If you spoke to her now, you spoke too soon."

"She has n't heard from her father yet," Hilgard said after a pause. "Is there no one to take care of her but that bedlam crew?"

"She *has* heard — she heard to-day. Her father's coming for her, and the minister's wife has found her out. She's a friendly little soul, with a lot of children." And then he added, "Remember, George, you can count on nature in the long run. I don't mean to flatter you, but did you ever ask anything of a woman and want it very much, and not get it?"

Hilgard flushed angrily.

"Do you call that flattering me? It is not a question of women, and it's not open to discussion."

"I'm done, boy — I'm done — only, just remember this: The worst thing that can happen to a man is to get some things, the best things, too easily."

"You've been my friend in a place where I haven't many," Hilgard said, relenting.

"You've had plenty of my kind. I tried to be your friend once, in a way that would have made you furious if you had known, but I didn't succeed."

"I don't know what you mean."

"I don't suppose you do. It's a pity I didn't succeed. However — Well, take care of yourself, boy! My feet are confoundedly damp."

Hilgard looked after the stout, stooping figure, shuffling away through the chilly streets, and the dull ache in his breast included older failures, and more hopeless ones, than his own. The world seemed full of them.

As he turned he saw West, who had ridden Peggy down from the mine, and stood near the post where she was hitched, waiting for Hilgard's recognition.

Peggy's toilet had been carefully attended to. The smoke from her silky sides rose in the cold air. It might have been the sickly gleam of the station lamps that gave West a pale, dragged look.

Hilgard slipped his hand under Peggy's mane, and patted her warm neck.

" You 'll see that they take good care of her, West."

" I will, sir. Peggy and me 'll leave the camp together."

" I don't mean anything of that sort. We have n't, either of us, any money to invest in sentiment."

" I know it, sir," said West, turning red. " But a man can fool himself with his own money, if he wants to. Peggy 's all the Led-Horse I want! I 'll take her for my two months' pay, if they 'll call it square!"

" You must n't do it, West! She is n't worth half of it. I 've used her hard, poor old girl! She was too light for my weight." He slid his hand down her fore leg, which she lifted obediently. "Her feet are all banged up. She needs a six weeks' run in the valley."

Peggy was smelling around Hilgard's pockets.

"Prospecting for sugar, Peggy? The sugar's in my other clothes. West, I wish you were going along."

"I wish so, too, sir."

"If I should find another job pretty soon, with decent pay, would you come with me? I don't want to interfere with your chances here."

"I ain't taking any chances here," said West, grimly. "They'll be havin' a new deal all round, when the next boss comes out. I'm going to quit before I'm kicked out."

"You're just as well out of it. It's an ugly camp. Gashwiler is not done with you."

"I expect not. Maybe I ain't done with him."

"You'd better get out of it, West! You're too good a man to be fooling with that kind of thing."

"Yes," said West. "They've got a notion in this camp that *fight's* all there is of me; but you know better than that, sir!"

"I should think I did. Well, look out for yourself!"

They shook hands silently.

As the train moved out of the depot, West stood with his arm across his saddle, his head hanging down.

"There ain't a man on top o' ground I 'd put up more on than him; I would n't wonder if he 'd know it some day," he muttered to himself; and, remounting Peggy, he rode away, through the snow-glimmer, under the dark, starlit sky.

Hilgard, looking from the car-window on the long grade descending toward the valley, saw the shrunken old moon crawl up above the notch of the Pass. A light glowed from the Led-Horse shaft-house, but the neighboring light across the gulch was out.

XII.

ON THE DOWN GRADE.

THE glittering snows of the Range melted into gray, soft showers as the eastward-bound train reached the valleys at its foot. The valleys opened and widened until, like rivers entering the sea, they were lost in the effacing levels of the plain.

At that season of dearth the brown plains of Colorado and Kansas were swept bare as threshing-floors, where the feet of wandering herds beat out the desert harvest, and the winds met at the winnowing, mocking the sterile crop and scattering it in wild eddies, mingled with the dust of the arid trails.

In a single night of travel the naked, titanic plains were changed for the rich savannas of Eastern Kansas, green with miles of sprouting wheat. For eyes tired with dust-laden winds and glare of lofty snow-fields, there was rest in this breadth of fertile country,

dimly seen through the rain-mist which was
gathering and trickling against the car-win-
dows.   To Hilgard's homesick gaze it looked
like the " lap of earth."

The rains continued. The deep, narrow
runs that go winding and looping through
the woods of Missouri were filling their dry,
summer channels from the low clouds.   It
was bright, windy weather crossing the rolling prairies of Iowa and the level prairies of
Illinois. Evening in Chicago was gray and
chill with the lake fogs ; but morning in the
valley of the Genesee was red with autumn
woods, and the broad, low light of the sun
shining through haze.

The " limited express " hurled itself into the
stillness of the landscape, giving it a dizzy,
panoramic movement ; the woods marched
like processions with banners along the horizon ; fields of standing corn, barns, fences,
villages, reeled past ; young girls in doorways,
groups of school-children, or men at work
in the fields, waved a greeting to the train,
and were left behind ; and, long after they
had gone their way, the figures and gestures
remained transfixed on the vision, like an
instantaneous photograph.

On that last day of his homeward journey, Hilgard watched the yellow twilight
reflected in the upper reaches of the Hudson.
The train dashed past the lights of river-
side hamlets and ferries; past little fleets of
sloops, creeping with the tide round a bend of
the river, and lazy communities of canal-boats
trailing behind the urgent propeller; past coun-
try-seats looking out from wooded knolls, and
farm-houses sheltered in the hollows; it came
clanging into the dingy depots of the river
cities. The familiar life roused him, like the
pang of returning consciousness, from the
dream-like succession of days and nights, set
to the monotonous, rhythmic jar of the car-
wheels pounding on the rails.

He entered New York with the daily incoming throng of summer tourists, returning from the sea, from the islands of the St.
Lawrence, from the mountains and lakes, —
from camping, yachting, hunting, and dancing. He registered his name at a hotel opposite one of those small, sunny parks where
summer in the city lingers longest, and appeared duly before a meeting of the Board of
Directors of the Led-Horse. The directors

found the situation an unexpected one; it was curious, it was even picturesque, and it implied an unhoped-for degree of prosperity in the future of the Led-Horse. Hilgard took his questioning very quietly. When the gentlemanly directors, finding, on reviewing the circumstances, that, in point of sentiment, a small deficit remained on their part, proposed its settlement with a check, Hilgard replied:—

"Gentlemen, you have paid me my salary as superintendent. I have simply been your superintendent, nothing more."

Hilgard had expected to lose no time on his return in looking up a new situation, and getting afield again; but he had not been prepared to find that the story of the fight in the drift had preceded him. The adventure met him everywhere among his acquaintances. It excited a certain enforced admiration, but it impressed the Eastern business mind as something excessive; as pitched not quite on the key of daily life.

Hilgard had known little of his native city since his boyhood; for at twenty he had gone to the Western frontier under the auspices of a government topographical survey. There

were links of old acquaintanceship and of
family that still held, through all his absences
and wanderings, but he hesitated, in his sick
and sore self-consciousness, from meeting familiar faces and subjecting himself to friendly
questioning.

He thought he would go down to that
quiet midland village where his half-brothers
were at school. He had seen very little of
them since their infancy, but they were en-
deared to him, not only for the sake of his
mother and theirs, but through grateful memories of their father, who had been his model
of manhood. Captain Norton's heroic and
untimely death at sea had been more of a
conscious loss to his step-son than to his own
baby-boys. The twice-widowed mother, whose
beauty, if it had brought her more than the
common share of love, had not saved her from
more than an equivalent of sorrow, had not
long survived this last blow.

The thought of these two lads, and of their
claim on his future, was, perhaps, the only one
at this time that Hilgard could dwell upon in
security from pain; and yet day after day
found him still in the city.

14

A deadly weariness, like nothing he had known, an apathy, as of premature age, had crept into the marrow of his bones, and taken from him his native instinct of resistance. He often found himself shivering in the soft fall sunshine. His thoughts seemed to swoon in the vacuum of his mind. He wondered indifferently if he could be ill ; he had never counted illness among the chances of his life, but he would have welcomed it, if he could have believed it would come quickly and forestall all future chances.

One evening, before the level sunset light had faded from the house-fronts, he was sitting on one of the benches in the little park, with his face turned away from the passers along the walks. He was meditating on that balance-sheet of sentiment between himself and the Led-Horse, and reviewing the events of the summer with a sickening doubt of his own action. People who paused to take a seat on the bench beside him, stared at him intently and passed on. Beautiful women and young girls, rustling by in rich fall costumes, looked back at him and whispered together. Little children, swinging from their nurse's hands, regarded him curiously; the gaunt shadows of the leafless trees that at noon were short on the asphalt walks, wheeled and lengthened softly over the turf. The sun dropped below the roofs; the shadows were diffused, and the after-glow mounted to the rows of upper-windows fronting the square. Gray twilight came down, and the myriad gas-jets started into life through all the purple vistas of streets, rising to meet the long, bright lanes of sky. A four-year-old child, loitering behind a white-capped maid, paused beside Hilgard's bench and laid a hand on his knee.

"What is the matter? Why don't you go home?"

The childish treble pierced Hilgard's dull mood, but he had no answer for the question. The maid returned in angry haste and hurried the child away.

Hilgard got upon his feet, stung by this involuntary tribute to his condition. Had he then become an object of such public commiseration that even the babes pitied him, and counselled him out of their wisdom of the nursery? He left the park and crossed the square, with an access of energy in his

·step ; but in the warm, gas-lit wilderness of
the hotel, his strength flagged suddenly. The
elevator was crowded with ladies, in street
toilets, ascending to their rooms. Hilgard
noticed, with vague surprise, that the tremulous upward motion made him giddy. In less
than a moment he reached the floor on which
his room was ; but to him it seemed he had
been standing a long time in the dimly lighted,
perfumed cell, with his eyes fixed on a reflection of the quivering chandelier in the polished
panel opposite, while women, whose draperies
crushed against him, talked to each other in
far-away voices, like those of a dream. He
staggered as he stepped into the corridor,
and apologized mechanically to a lady whom
he had jostled.

She appeared to be a newly arrived traveller,
waiting for the call-boy with her hand-luggage
to show her to her room. She had a sensitive face, of a type we instinctively refer to
pictures of a by-gone generation of faces. She
looked at Hilgard earnestly, as he lifted his
hat and muttered his apology ; and with a
slight, nervous blush, appealed to him in her
momentary annoyance.

"I think I have mistaken the floor my room is on. The boy was to meet me at the elevator with my things and show me to fifty-six."

"Fifty-six is on this floor, madam, — I am going that way."

The lady hesitated, as if she felt under some obligation to wait for the call-boy, and then followed Hilgard along the hall. He tried to keep the number in his mind ; the succession of white doors, with gilded numerals on them, swam before his eyes; the hall seemed endless, and the floor to rise and sink under his feet like the deck of a ship. He stopped, and steadied himself against the wall.

"Why, here it is! thank you very much!" the lady said, in a tone of relief. At that moment a door on the opposite side of the hall unclosed, and the shock of a sudden heartbreaking recognition roused Hilgard like a blow in the face. Cecil Conrath had opened the door of fifty-six, and stood the width of the corridor away from him, looking into his face with the blank gaze of a stranger.

The little lady made an exclamatory rush forward, and the door was shut. Hilgard stood a moment staring at the number outside it, and then went to his own room. He made an effort to light the gas, groped about helplessly, and sank down in a chair, the blood heavily surging in his veins. It ebbed wave by wave, and his life seemed ebbing with it, in slower and slower pulsations.

The servant, coming in a few minutes later with a pitcher of ice-water, found him, in the dim light that streamed into the room from the transom, lying back in his chair, white and senseless.

XIII.

NUMBER FIFTY-TWO.

THAT part of his journey to the mountain camp which had reference to his daughter, had not given Mr. Conrath much uneasiness beforehand. He thought of her as little more than a child, to be petted into forgetfulness of the shock she had suffered. He did not know how fully Cecil might be acquainted with the circumstances of her brother's death, and he avoided any allusion to the subject; at the same time he resented her unyouthful silence, and the absence of all appeal on her part to the paternal refuge.

Cecil was not aware of the reproachful power of her grief. The effort by which she had set every strained and quivering nerve to its silent endurance had left her no strength for self-analysis or for comprehension of another's phases of feeling. As for help in her trial, she would sooner have asked the prayers of the

church for one whose burden was heavier
than she could bear, than have appealed to
that automatic relation which was all she had
ever known of fatherhood.

When Mr. Conrath proposed to find a suit-
able escort for her on her homeward journey,
and to remain himself a week longer in the
camp, for the purpose of investigating an interest his son was said to have had in some
presumably valuable, though undeveloped,
mining properties, Cecil gave a listless assent.
It was arranged that she should travel in
company with a lady experienced in railway
journeys, opportunely going east, as far as
Chicago, and be met in New York by her
mother's sister, Miss Esther Hartwell. At
the hotel selected by Mr. Conrath they were
to await his return and his subsequent plans
for Cecil's future home.

Home! — the very word seemed to mock
the fragmentary, wistful existence which had
been her life since early childhood.

Mr. Conrath's enforced stay in the camp was
prolonged from day to day, while Miss Esther
silently repined at her life of idleness, with her
fall sewing yet undone, in a city full of men

and women, all overworking or overplaying —
while Cecil listened to every footstep along
the hall, and paled or flushed expectantly,
growing daily more restless with the haunting
thought of Hilgard near, yet never seen.·

Ten days had passed, and Hilgard had
been sinking deeper, day by day, in that
rift of oblivion into which he had fallen.
The tide of movement in the city set south-
ward in the morning and northward at night,
through the shrill echoing channels of its
streets. There were inquirers for him among
Hilgard's acquaintances, but they answered
each other that he had gone out of town,
probably, on that visit to his brothers, which
he had mentioned among his earliest inten-
tions. He lay, drifting fast toward the crisis
of his strength.

"Cecil, do you know we have a case of
fever in our hall?"
Miss Esther had gathered the information
from scraps of talk in the elevator during the
day's ascendings and descendings, and con-
firmed it through the medium of one of the
chamber-maids. " It is only two doors from

us, — fifty-two. No one comes to see him, Ellen says, except the Doctor; and he has a hired nurse."

Miss Esther Hartwell was from the country, and classed hired nurses with baker's bread and shop-made underclothing, and other desolations which properly belonged with the homeless existence of people who lived in hotels and boarding-houses.

"It's been running more than a week, now," Miss Esther continued; "they say he has typhoid symptoms, if it isn't the real thing. It seems as if I couldn't sit here, day after day, with my hands folded!"

Miss Esther was not literally sitting with her hands folded; on the contrary, her active habits were asserting themselves on a circuit of the room, for the purpose of softly dispersing, with a hare's-foot brush, the faint gray dust-films which had settled on the ornaments and carvings. The puffs of hair laid against her temples looked as if a faint gray film had settled on them too, but it had come gradually, and would not be brushed away until the finger of time should obliterate the gentle picture, of which it was now an essential part.

It would be as impossible to think of Miss Esther without her soft, prim side-puffs, as without her gold eyeglasses, with their slender, worn rims, or the delicate depressions around her mouth and nostrils.

Cecil was standing at the window, with her back to her aunt, her elbows resting on the low sash, her head bowed between her hands until her forehead touched the cool window-pane.

Miss Esther was accustomed to Cecil's long silences; she thought the girl brooded too much, but she remembered her own youth, and youth's passionate preoccupation with its own troubles. She had not expected from Cecil much demonstration of interest in that forlorn sick-room, which appealed so strongly to her own experienced sympathies.

" I 've known cases," Miss Esther meditated, aloud, " where they slipped away just at the turn, for want of some one who would n't give up hope. There are always plenty who will say, ' Oh, let him rest — let him draw his last breath in peace ! ' but then is the time not to think of rest."

Miss Esther shut the brush away in the

drawer of a side-table, and stood with her back against it, still wrestling with the helpful impulse, of which she was half ashamed, as we are apt to be of gratuitous impulses of that kind. Her eyeglass fell, and tinkled softly against the buttons of her dress.

" Have you thought of offering to help nurse him, Aunt Esther ? " Cecil asked.

" Anywhere but here I should n't stop to think about it, — I should go right in ! " Miss Esther replied with energy. " After all, suppose he *is* a stranger," she argued with her own doubts, — " he 's our neighbor in one sense. I 'm ashamed to pass that door, and never even ask if there is anything I can do."

Cecil came and stood beside Miss Esther, half-embracing her, and crushing her firm young cheek, in which a sympathetic glow had begun to brighten, against Miss Esther's side-combs.

" You are good enough to do things you feel like doing, without stopping to think. You would do it at Little Rest?"

" At Little Rest! " Miss Esther repeated, — " this is n't much like Little Rest ! Here, it is the first law for every one to mind his own business. I can't get it out of my mind, Cecil, that he is the same young man I met in the hall the night I çame. He looked so strange! I said to myself then, either he's stricken with some sickness or —" (Cecil looked at her aunt fixedly, while the arrested blush faded from her face) — "or else he's been drinking!" Miss Esther concluded, in an undertone, burdened by the gravity of this last hypothesis.

"He might have been sick or dying, but he was not *that!*" Cecil said. She stood before Miss Esther, and put out her hands with a pleading gesture.

"Will you go to him now! Don't stop to think any longer. What does it matter where we are? Ah — *go!*" she entreated in her sudden unaccountable excitement.

"Why, Cecil, do you care so much?" Miss Esther was bewildered by the girl's mood, but she had ever a gentle construction for all moods but her own, and found in this only an occasion for self-reproach. She took the young girl into her arms and let the convulsed face hide itself against her shoulder.

"Your heart is sore, poor child; too sore to bear anybody's pain! I haven't understood you; I thought you were wrapped up in your own trouble!"

"This — this is my trouble!" Cecil confessed, helplessly.

"Don't make too much of it, dear. I'm sorry I told you. After all, he *is* a stranger!"

"I hope he is; but, you *must* find out his name!"

Miss Esther had left the room and arrived at the neighboring door of number fifty-two, scarcely conscious of the steps which had taken her there; but once inside that door, face to face with an extremity of need, which she recognized at a glance, her perturbation was stilled by that active sense of power the true nurse feels in the presence of such need.

On her return to her own room, an hour later, she found Cecil lying on the bed, her eyes shut, her clasped hands close huddled beneath her chin.

Miss Esther softly drew up the coverlet over the motionless figure.

"I'm not asleep," Cecil said, opening her eyes. She kept them on Miss Esther's face, intently searching its expression. "What is his name?" she asked.

An intuition had come to Miss Esther during her absence which made it hard for her to answer. She sat down by the bed and laid her head by Cecil's on the pillow. The girl did not repeat her question, but her hand wandered with a beseeching touch toward the face beside her own. Miss Esther took the hand and held it fast while she said, in the same hushed voice she had used in the sick-room, —

"It is a strange thing. He is that — Hilgard!"

The imprisoned hand closed quickly within her own and then relaxed. Cecil turned her face away.

"Did you know him, Cecil?"

"Yes."

"Child, what can there be between him and Harry Conrath's sister?"

"Nothing; but I may wish him not to die."

Cecil lay, dull-eyed and silent, while Miss Esther stroked her unresponsive hand. Suddenly she withdrew it, and, rising on her elbow in the bed, demanded, —

"What have you heard about him?"

"I have heard only what your father wrote me."

"My father will never know the whole story; he knows — only one cruel thing!"

Cecil sank back on her pillow again, pressing her hands hard over her eyes.

"It is no use! I could never make you understand — no one will ever understand! Oh, why are men put in such places?"

She tossed her arms wide apart upon the bed, turning a look of suffering past all concealment upon the woman who was nearest to her.

"I love him," she whispered, in all that was left of her choked utterance. "I could not take happiness from him — but now — now I may go to him! Now I can be merciful."

"Hush, my poor child! Mercy is not in your hands," Miss Esther said. "He is very young — he is very sick," she added, simply, as if in further extenuation.

"But he was *not* to blame!" Cecil started up again, and slipped from the bed to the floor, beginning, with trembling hands, instinctively to coil up her loosened braids. "I am going to him. It cannot do any harm.

He shall know — " She stopped, arrested by a new and sickening doubt. "Aunt Esther, have you told me all ? "

" My dear, there is not much to tell. He is very low. You must not expect him to know you. It is the same to him who comes or goes."

Cecil received this blow in silence. She wavered in restless circles, like a broken-winged bird, around the room, and settled despairingly at last at Miss Esther's knee.

" You will help him just the same, now you know who he is ? "

" Help him ? Why, Cecil, what kind of a woman do you think I am ? "

" Oh, I know ! It is only I who can do such things. I let him go away that night without a sign. You saw he needed help. It was cruel to shut the door in his face."

" Why, if you mean that night in the hall, *I* shut the door, Cecil. I remember — "

" Won't you go back to him now ? " Cecil interrupted. " You have been a long time away. It will do no good for me to go, but I must — I must see him ! "

Miss Esther yielded reluctantly to Cecil's

15

desire. The relation between Hilgard and
her niece seemed too unreal, and, under the
late circumstances, too unnatural to be admitted. Miss Esther, as Cecil had guessed,
only knew concerning Hilgard the one fact
of the fatal conjunction of his name with that
of her nephew. Mr. Conrath had written
only enough to forestall rumor. He had
neither defended his son nor accused Hilgard,
but the simple fact of his death left Conrath
master of sympathies that were already his by
the tie of kinship, and had never been alienated by intimate knowledge of his character.

But Cecil's grief was not to be gainsaid.
It was the more impressive from the silence
that had preceded this sudden outburst of its
smothered pain.

The two women went together along the
corridor to the door of the sick-room. Miss
Esther met the nurse, who admitted them
with a few words of explanation, while Cecil,
heeding no one, stared with dread into the
gloom of the cool, shaded room.

The tenant of fifty-two lay sunk on a white,
thinly-clad bed, the lines of his long form
showing beneath the folds of the coverlid,

like a carved effigy on a tomb. One hand,
stretched by his side, stirred slightly, but the
profile outlined against the swell of the pillow
was as immobile as a death-mask. Cecil went
to him and cowered on the floor beside him,
sparing her shrinking sight not one detail of
the change. She crept close to the bed and
laid her white cheek in the hollow of his dry,
wasted hand. Her breath came in hard, tear-
less sobs. She gazed within the parted lids,
where a dull, sightless glimmer remained.
There was no recognition; no need for her
to shrink where there was no importunity; to
resist where argument and appeal had ceased.
His estate, now, was less than her own. The
ruined tenement which had been his house of
life was void and silent, welcoming no one,
disputing no intrusion.

Though she had judged and sentenced him,
she had held him blameless. She worshipped
the steadfastness with which he had turned
back to his barren post of duty in the face of
a young man's last temptation. Who would
ever understand, in the world of peace and
order, that wild summons which had forced
an instant's choice upon him! and where

would peace and order be found, if there were no men to obey when such a summons came! And she had made him feel that they were forever aliens by this deed.

"My brother," she whispered, "my two brothers! God judge between you, and let me call you both mine!"

A small clock on the mantel ticked breathlessly, as if hurrying on the moments to the long silence on the threshold of which she knelt. In that sudden collapse of hope which youth can know, she felt that he was already gone. She could not conceive that a change so terrible might not be final.

Miss Esther went to her and with gentle insistence drew her away. At the door Cecil looked back as one who has laid a last flower on the bosom of the dead.

Miss Esther watched for the Doctor's evening visit, and, when his examination of the patient was over, she proffered her help for the night-watch in a low-voiced conversation with him outside the sick-room door. Her quaint earnestness was mingled with a practical efficiency which the Doctor recognized and readily availed himself of. At the close

of their talk he alluded to the young lady
visitor of whom the nurse had told him.

" A friend of the patient's ? " he asked.

" She is my niece, Doctor," Miss Esther
replied. The Doctor did not fail to note the
evasion and her flush of embarrassment.

" The patient is a relative of yours, did I
understand you to say, or of your niece ? "

" He is not a relative, Doctor ; I have no
excuse for offering my help — "

" Except the best of excuses, madam, —
that your help is needed. Mrs. Wren inferred
that our patient and the young lady were not
strangers to each other ; does she propose to
offer her assistance, too ? "

" No, Doctor, — the patient is not a stranger to us, but my niece has no idea of helping
to nurse him."

" Well, you know, it might n't be altogether
a bad idea. There might be circumstances
that would make her presence, at least, a
most fortunate thing for the case. I confess
I counted on more resistance on the patient's
part to the progress of the disease. There
would be no need for volunteers by this time,
if the case had developed as I expected. With

his physique and at his age I did n't antici-
pate the least trouble. I 'm inclined to think
there has been some shock or strain that 's
telling against him now. The fact is, it
struck me from the first that he was n't particularly anxious to get well."

Miss Esther was silent a moment, and then,
as the Doctor appeared to wait for her to
speak, she said : —

"From what I know of him, I should n't
think he would be."

"But why should n't he? As far as one
can judge by the outside of a man, he is well
fitted to live."

"Oh, Doctor, there has been trouble!"
Miss Esther admitted, desperately.

"I supposed so. He appears to have something on his mind. It 's often a very obstinate
feature — the mind, you know. Mrs. Wren
said the young lady appeared to be a good
deal affected by the patient's condition. Was
it with a particular interest in him she came
in to see him? It 's — well — a little unusual,
you know, unless there 's some previous relation. This trouble you speak of — is it a common trouble — I mean a mutual trouble?"

" Yes, Doctor," Miss Esther replied, blushing with a sense of the responsibility imposed upon her. " It is partly mutual — that is — I'm not really in her confidence, but he is a great deal to her. I am sure of that. It is a shock to her to see him like this. I don't know what influence she may have over him — "

The Doctor smiled, as if to lighten Miss Esther's sense of the awfulness of her disclosure.

" Those things are often reciprocal, you know, Madam. Is your niece's name Cecil, by the way ? "

Miss Esther assented in surprise.

" The patient has mentioned that name. He wanders a little at times — can't get the number fifty-six out of his mind." The Doctor glanced casually up at the door opposite.

" That is the number of our room," Miss Esther explained.

" Well, Madam, if there is no serious objection, I wish the patient could see your niece, quietly, you know, when he seems to be conscious. It may be another chance in his favor."

"I don't see what my niece can do for him, Doctor — except deceive him," said Miss Esther, with shrinking conscientiousness.

" Our business, Madam, is to get him well. He must take care of himself afterward."

About nine o'clock Miss Esther began her night toilet in preparation for watching instead of sleeping. She took out her tortoise-shell side-combs and rolled up her puffs into little flat rings against her temples and fastened each with a hair-pin. She substituted a warm wrapper for her rustling dress, and drew on a pair of noiseless knitted shoes. She wound her watch, and gave it a little shake before trusting to its good faith; then, in the silence of her own room, she murmured to herself the first verses of the psalm beginning: "Except the Lord build the house, they labor in vain that build it; except the Lord keep the city, the watchman waketh but in vain." And, in the familiar words, she commended her labors of the night to the source of all her modest courage.

There was one more duty to perform. She went to the bed where Cecil lay in a stupor of hopeless grief.

" Cecil, my dear, the Doctor thinks we may
need your help. Not to-night, perhaps, but
you must be ready. You must not go to bed
without food, if it's only a glass of milk.
And you need not waste your strength mourning for that young man while he is living.
Better save it to help him keep alive!"

Miss Esther had seldom spoken to better
purpose, but she did not wait to see the effect
of her words.

Morning, when it came, found the watchers
hopeful.

Limp as sea-weed forsaken by the tide,
Hilgard lay waiting for the returning wave of
life to uplift and outspread the draggled filaments of his consciousness. The tide was
creeping back; at dawn it floated him off
into a sleep like that of a new-born babe,
from which he woke scarcely less weak than
one, to rest his eyes on the face of Cecil
Conrath.

During his waking hours, all that first day
of hope, his large-eyed gaze followed her with
a mute surmise. She was always silent, but
there was a mysterious joy in her face which
puzzled him; he could not connect it with

himself. The appeal in his eyes grew sharper with his strengthening pulse, until, wearied with this fair, unanswering apparition of a forbidden hope, he turned away from it, and tears of baffled weakness stole from under his closed lids. Cecil laid her cool touch upon his wrist, and held it there until he turned his head toward her again, and, lifting his eyes, faintly formed the words, —

" Why did you wish me to live ?"

She withdrew her hand, but steadily meeting his eyes, with that primal question in them, answered, —

" Because I could not die, too."

He continued to gaze at her, as if pondering her words, and trying if their meaning would stretch to the limit of his reviving longing. Cecil bent her head low, to hide the wild-rose color that bloomed suddenly in her cheeks.

" You are going to get well, for my sake," she said.

This was Cecil's deception.

No renunciation could have been quieter or more absolute in intention than hers, when she resolved that the way should not be left open for Hilgard's love to follow her when she left him again.

Her father returned, and robbed her meek sacrifice of its dignity by making it no longer voluntary.

Mr. Conrath had no sympathy with any form of practical Christianity which took the women of his family into the sick-rooms of pilgrims and strangers. He found an absolute incompatibility between Miss Esther's spirit of promiscuous helpfulness and her chaperonage of his daughter. But, when the name of the patient transpired, Mr. Conrath permitted himself a vigorous use of language in characterizing this feminine crusade. He was under no illusions as to the part his son had taken in the collision between the Led-Horse and the Shoshone; the facts made it undeniably hard for Conrath's father to be magnanimous, since he was scarcely in a position to forgive Hilgard for defending the trust in his keeping from his son's rapacity; but he did not propose that his daughter should be the hostage of his future relations with the knight of the Led-Horse.

Cecil was at once called upon to decide between two alternatives, either of which would remove her from her undesirable proximity. The choice lay between Havana and her stepmother's company, and her grandmother Hartwell's house at Little Rest. Without hesitation, Cecil chose to go down into the country with Miss Esther to Little Rest.

She doubted long, on the eve of her departure, — watching the night through, in weary tossings, — whether to go away without a sign, or trust herself to one last expression of her love to soften the fact of her desertion.

When Hilgard awoke the next day from one of his long, restoring sleeps, a familiar perfume stole luxuriously upon his languid senses. The nurse brought to his bedside a bunch of long-stemmed, heavy-headed roses, and a note which had lain neighbor to them long enough to borrow a hint of their fragrance. But it carried its own sting, keener than the sharpest of their healthy thorns. It was hastily written in pencil, in the hand Hilgard had seen once before, when Cecil had bidden him to that forlorn tryst in the gulch.

The words of the note had been the result of Cecil's native necessity to be honest. "If

it does harm," she had said to herself, worn out with self-conflict, "I cannot help it. I will give up everything, but he shall know that I love him." She wrote: —

"My father has returned, and we leave town to-day. You must get well. I shall know, though I never see you, that your life will justify my love and faith. You need not try to find me. We are not for each other in this world."

Cecil's love had not enlightened her very deeply concerning the character of her lover, if she could imagine him restored to what he had been when she had first seen him, and yet passive under her gentle proscription. It served, however, as the tonic which his will required. It stung him into a passionate resolve to get control once more of that good servant, his body, with which he had so lately been willing to part company.

XIV.

LITTLE REST.

" WHY was it called ' Little Rest '? " Cecil asked, as the carriage slowly climbed the hill from the station. She had known the name since childhood, but its familiarity had dulled her ear to its meaning, which struck her now for the first time.

" It was a half-way stopping place for the stages on the old post road," Miss Esther replied. " They changed horses at Sullivan, two miles on. This long hill was hard for the tired horses ; they used to stop at the foot of the first rise to water and breathe them a little. First there was a blacksmith's shop, and a box on the side of the big elm for letters and papers ; then there was a tavern called ' The Little Rest.' "

Cecil softly repeated the name to herself. The horses dropped into a steady, hard-pulling walk, after their first spurt up the long, steep grade, which was broken at intervals by shallow, transverse hollows to lead off the water.

The Hartwell house stood at the end of a broad, grass-grown lane which joined the main road at the top of the hill. Cecil's memories of her grandmother's house went back when she was just tall enough to see her face, distorted in miniature reflection, in the polished brass door-knobs; when, to her small stride, the meadow-grass in June was a tropical jungle, and a seat among the low apple-tree boughs in the orchard had seemed from the ground a perilous adventure.

In those days she had found it a long walk from the white-painted gate-posts up the straight drive to the high-pillared porch. The house had been built during the white wooden temple period of domestic architecture, which belonged to the early eighteen hundreds. Its formal lines were repeated in those of the leafless locust-trees, facing each other, on either side of the drive, in a stately expectancy — as of the arrival of some guest who never came, or the passing of bridal carriages, or a funeral procession from the white-panelled front-door beneath the

porch. This fancy occurred to Cecil looking
from the window of the hack, which had
stopped before the closed gate. The driver
called to a man who was raking the dead
leaves into heaps upon the withered grass
of the door-yard. He was an elderly man,
and he came deliberately, first hooking his
rake in the low boughs of a tree. He put
his shoulder under the top bar of the gate
and lifted it on its hinges, before swinging
it open. As the carriage passed through,
he stood aside and nodded silently in response
to Miss Esther's greeting.

The years since Cecil had seen them last
had thinned the ranks of the locusts. Here
and there a comrade had dropped out of
line; the loss of their close-set, plumy foliage
suffered the amputation of limbs to be seen.
A few faded leaves clung to the boughs, or
drifted downward in the still air, falling as
light as the first snow-flakes would soon fall
on the shrunken turf. The rose-bushes in
the beds beneath the front windows were
swathed in straw, and bowed with their
heads to the earth, and the cords which had
sustained their blossoming sprays in summer,

hung slack and rain-bleached against the side of the house.

Miss Esther straightened the door-mat with her foot, before entering. She did not knock, but the heavy door stuck slightly, and opened with a jar which set the brass knocker's teeth a-chattering.

The interior of the hall was darkened by faded green silk shades drawn down over the side-lights. The slender mahogany stair-rail made a square turn at the landing, and, continuing upward, caught a strong gleam of pure white light from an uncurtained window above. A tall closet opened on the landing. Cecil remembered how her brother had been wont to conceal himself there and spring out upon her unawares, on her toilsome journeys up and down the staircase, with a doll under each arm, and a doll's wardrobe in a broken bandbox in her hands. She had never, as a child, been able to pass that closet without thrills of acute terror; even when the doors stood ajar, the long, dark garments hanging within had been invested to her imagination with the mystery of which they were the sole proprietors.

16

Martha, the respectable "help," warned by the involuntary noise of their entrance, met them at the door of the back parlor, and informed them that Mrs. Hartwell was in her own room dressing after her afternoon nap. She looked deliberately and curiously at Cecil, glanced at the hard-coal fire to see if it required mending, asked Miss Esther some commonplace question about their journey, and then retired to the region of the kitchen.

The two women, left alone, were silent; Cecil gazed about her, taking in the details of the room, with shocks of recollection, and Miss Esther followed wistfully the expression of her face. The presence of a young girl in the house made her realize its subdued life and remoteness, and the lapse of time since her own girlhood.

A slow, heavy step was heard moving about overhead.

"I will go up and see mother," Miss Esther said, " and see if your room is ready."

Cecil turned toward her aunt with a quick, affectionate gesture.

"Everything is just as it used to be — only then I did not know how lovely it was! If you only *knew* how different it is!"

" Different ? "

" From other places I have known."

" Ah, my dear, if you had only come to us last summer ! "

Cecil did not echo this wish; she could hardly have told why. She had put off her hat and wraps, and knelt before the fire as she had often knelt in the glow of the great stone chimney of the Shoshone cabin.

" I must be content ! " she adjured her failing heart, on the threshold of this new life of peace.

There was a rustle of thin silk behind her, as the door opened and her grandmother entered. She greeted Cecil very quietly, almost coldly, and, to her exquisite relief, made no allusion to the circumstances connected with her present visit to Little Rest. She took the chair on the opposite side of the fire, rocking gently, while her eyes dwelt on Cecil's face with a prolonged and retrospective gaze. Her white, withered hands, with the purplish veins showing on their backs, were crossed over her pocket handkerchief, and rested on the ample slope which the folds of her black satin apron took in their descent toward her lap.

Clear white muslin bands encircled her wrists.

The placid figure, the creak of the chair in its brief oscillations, the tinkle of a coal falling on the iron pan beneath the grate, had for Cecil a fascinating, dreamy familiarity. In the plain slab of black marble which crossed the chimney-piece, there was a darkly reflected picture of the room, in the fading light. Miss Esther was laying the cloth for tea, and placing the gilt china and the thin, bent-edged silver tea-service in order. As a child, Cecil had often watched this same picture from her seat on the embroidered footstool, which was decorated with a pink-eyed lamb, whose outlines, year by year, became more confused with the green and buff landscape in which its feet were set. Even the strip of orange-colored sky showing behind the thin woods on the hill, looked in through the window with a friendly light. Her childhood seemed waiting, with gentle, appealing touches of memory, to heal the wounds that womanhood had given her.

When Mrs. Hartwell spoke to Cecil of her brother, it was always of the little boy she had known long ago. The events of his life subsequent to that time she ignored, as if he had died in childhood. Cecil sometimes wondered at this silence, but she accepted it, and was unspeakably grateful for it. It was a silence which covered more than the proud old heart would have permitted any one to guess. Grandmamma Hartwell had been enlightened in various ways as to Harry Conrath's development, since the days of his childish sovereignty over the household at Little Rest. As a trifling incident of this development, he had borrowed sums of money of her from time to time, making little filial journeys down into the country for that purpose. Miss Esther had often recalled these visits with the pathetic appreciation with which elderly retired gentlewomen dwell upon the disinterested attentions of their young male relatives.

Mrs. Hartwell had received the news of her grandson's death with outward composure, but for many days she had been strangely restless. She had seemed more heavy and silent since that time Only once had she alluded to the family grief. This was on the

evening before Miss Esther's journey to New
York to meet Cecil.   Miss Esther had come
into her mother's room to cover her fire and
arrange her for the night.   The old lady was
sitting up in bed in her nightcap, with a
loose, wadded silk sack over her night-dress.
She seemed nervous, and watched Miss
Esther's movements with impatience.

"Why don't you let Martha attend to the
fire? She does it perfectly well. What is
the use of making your hands rough for
nothing at all except a fancy that I'm more
comfortable for it. I'm not. I can't bear to
see you on your knees before that grate."

"Martha can do it when I'm away," Miss
Esther replied, mildly.

When she came to the bedside to say good-
night, her mother detained her by the hand.

"Sit down a minute, Essie. Put that
shawl around you."   Mrs. Hartwell did not
speak again, immediately. She was rolling up
her cap-string, and her fingers were slightly
tremulous.   "I don't suppose he would let you
bring her down here," she said, presently.

"He didn't say anything about it; but of
course he couldn't say anything in a tele-

gram. Perhaps there will be a letter — or
she may know what he wants her to do."

"He cannot want to keep her in that hotel!
Strange ways! Strange ways!" the old lady
repeated.

"He always seemed to be afraid the children would get — well — our ways," said Miss
Esther. "I know he thinks we are very provincial down here."

"He did n't seem to think your sister was
provincial — before he married her." After a
moment's silence, Mrs. Hartwell spoke again,
in her deep voice. "Where is that picture,
Essie, — that picture of Harry?"

"Mother, I put it away. I thought it
would hurt you to see it all the time."

"People have to get used to being hurt. I
wish you 'd bring it back."

XV.

OLD PATHWAYS.

CECIL had not been brought up in the
habit of industry. To sit perfectly still and
unemployed for an hour at a time was no
affliction to her, as it would have been to
Miss Esther — as it undeniably was to Miss
Esther to see her thus listlessly drifting, day
after day, with the tide of her thoughts.
She spoke to her mother on the subject of
her duty to the young girl in this respect, but
Grandmamma Hartwell replied : —

"Let her alone for a while. She does n't
look like one who needs spurring."

Cecil was never troubled by the long gaze
which her grandmother would often fix upon
her, as they sat opposite each other by the
fire. She made no attempt to respond to it.
It seemed to pass beyond her own personality, and to recall, in her face and movements,
other faces and older histories than hers.

But she was happier with her grandmother than with Miss Esther, whose hovering solicitude fretted her and increased her self-consciousness. Her spirit gradually keyed itself to the subdued monotone of the eventless days, succeeding each other with the soft, obliterating effect of dropping water. The sharpness of her pain subsided into a mental torpor which forbade either hope or passionate repining. It would have been premature to call it resignation.

Cecil did not look unhappy in these days, but she was not able to bear the house-life without long, solitary walks which had the effect, almost, of a voluntary religious exercise.

On rainy days, she would stand at the windows of the cold, unused parlor, and watch the locust-trees rock and strain in the wind; with them, in spirit, she rode out the storm. At twilight she was able to take her place at the piano, whose keys had a thin, sweet tinkle, like the melodies that had been played on it in its prime. The folding-doors were parted, that her grandmother, sitting by the fire in the back parlor, might listen to "Joys that

we 've tasted," and " Believe me, if all those
endearing young charms," until Martha came
in with the lamp and announced that supper
was ready.

Cecil had found a succession of harmonies
that fitted the words, —

> " Oh, me, oh, me ! what frugal cheer
> My love doth feed upon,"

and sometimes in moments of weakness she
gave them utterance, enunciating the perilous
syllables softly, with a sense of self-betrayal
and of tampering with resolution.

Fair days or cloudy always found her
a-field, climbing the brown orchard slope behind the house and fleetly following the path
which led down through the gap in the stone
fence to the level meadows, below the mill-
dam. It was a country of abrupt heights and
hollows; in the spring, the half-hidden water-
courses made a pleasant noise among the
hills, but only the greater streams survived
the summer.

Cecil's accustomed way took her across the
mill-dam by the well-worn path. The leafless willows crossed their red-tipped lances in

the sun above her head. On one side lay
the glassy pond, and, below the wall of the
dam, the shorn meadow, with a faint new
greenness showing along the course of the
waste-water from the dam. The path rose
abruptly, beyond the mill-dam, and disappeared on the wooded hill which bounded the
eastern shore of the pond. There were no
long outlooks here, but there was seclusion
and peace in the narrow boundaries of the
horizon. The sky limits were confined; there
was no mystery of far-off line of sea or
estranging plain. The hills were near neighbors; their language was content rather than
aspiration.

Cecil's most frequent refuge was the wood.
Here her restless footsteps were stayed; she
waded into its rustling hollows, deep in fallen
leaves; she stood and listened to its still-
nesses. Often she would throw herself down,
like a burden she was weary of, on its broad,
brown lap, letting her eyes travel upward to
the complex tracery of tree-stems screening
the sky, as a sick child will dully follow the
pattern of its mother's dress or the reflections
in her bending eyes.

Yet she could be merry at times, when
other young voices were near, to catch and
repeat the fitful note of gayety in her own.
The young voices that sometimes echoed with
hers through the wood belonged to two bright-
faced lads of twelve and fourteen years, who
appeared to enjoy more liberty than usually
falls to the lot of schoolboys. They were
the only boarding-pupils in the family of the
minister, who kept a private school in the
neighborhood. When the afternoon sunlight
gilded the tree-stems and dappled the warm
slopes of the wood, they were always at large,
making the rounds of their favorite haunts;
visiting their quail-snares and rabbit-traps, or
the chestnut-trees, where the last of the crop
lay under the leaves, or extending their circuit to the neighboring fields in search of
frozen-thawed apples. Divers and many were
their errands, but none of so pressing a nature
that time was wanting for wrestling together
in beds of fallen leaves or flinging surrep-
titious armfuls of them over each other, or
pausing on the top rail of a fence that crossed
a hill, to wake the silent landscape with a
shrill hoot or whistle.

By little and little, in odd ways, a shy, wary comradeship had sprung up between this light-hearted pair and the lonely girl. She took no particular attitude toward them; she was not motherly or sisterly or cousinly; she was not even invariably friendly. Her mood could not be foretold. Sometimes she would pass them with an abstracted smile; for days, perhaps, they would not exchange a word; then an afternoon would find them following, side by side, the obscure highways of the wood, or seated in the shelter of a rock, or on some dry hill-slope, munching sweet withered chestnuts and talking idly, while the shadows crept past them before the low sun.

In the early stages of their acquaintance, Cecil was not greatly interested in the lads as individuals. She liked their impersonal boyhood; their calls to each other across intervening hills; their ambuscades and sallies and notes of warning, their unexpected touches of rude sentiment; the listening look in their faces, and the unconscious, perpetual play of life in their slim, restless bodies. But her observation of them was

respectful and reticent. They were vaguely
stimulated by it, though its outward signs
were slight. Her companionship was a unique
experience in the lives of the two boys. Her
indefinite, girlish loveliness and grace of silence or of speech, the unexplained solitude
of her musing walks, some hint of melancholy
which they dimly felt in her presence as they
felt the thrill in the note of the hermit-thrush
in the heart of the spring woods, touched that
dumb response to beauty which, in a boy's
nature, is often hidden in proportion to its
strength. To each other they seldom spoke
of Cecil, and by a tacit understanding, when
they were attended by their schoolmates, they
avoided her company, as a pleasure too fine
to be indiscriminately shared.

Cecil was as incurious about the actual
life and character of her two comrades as
if she had been a veritable nymph or dryad
of the woods, meeting them on that border-
land of enchantment which tradition supplies
for such mythical companionships. She heard
them call each other Bert and Charley, and
she inferred from their accent and bearing
that their associations had been gentle and

their discipline scant. They had read with youthful avidity and promiscuously, like boys who had had books within reach, with no one to guide their selection.

She had no distinct preference for Bert, but when she talked to both boys, she looked in his face more often than in Charley's. Bert's eyes were dark, and his strongly marked eye-brows descended slightly as they approached each other; when his hat was pushed back, his thick, brown forelock showed below the brim; his nose was still uncertain in shape. He laughed a great deal, showing his big, solid, white teeth between lips whose curves kept their childlike purity of outline. His face was deeply, richly colored; the rims of his well-formed ears glowed a fine crimson against the slope of close-shorn hair fading into the lighter brown of his neck. Charley, the elder lad, was blonde and freckled. He had an honest, sensitive countenance, and eyes which needed only darker shading in the brows and lashes to bring out their beauty; but Charley's good looks were problematical, while Bert's were in transition.

It was not, however, its joyous beauty that

drew Cecil's eyes so often to Bert's face; it was a puzzling, elusive hint which came and went, with its changing expressions, of another face she had known. The fascination of its recurrence grew upon her unawares; she watched for it, and yet shrank from it when it returned. It was an innocent, unaccountable likeness; its little intermittent hurt could hardly be said to trouble a peace that was not yet attained, or to rouse memories that had never slept.

Early in December, the thin, gray ice that stilled the surface of the pond grew strong enough to bear skaters. The quiet of the neighboring hills was invaded by a confusion of voices and the echoes of steel-shod feet treading the sounding ice-floor. A light, dry snow fell, whitening the pathways of the wood. It disappeared quickly from the open fields, but lingered, like sifted ashes, on the brown leaves in the wooded hollows.

Cecil had found a new revelation of half-forgotten beauty in the white precincts of the pond, lying, like water in a swoon, beneath the bright, unfruitful winter skies. She was still attended by her juvenile body-guard, nor

did she covet other company. Quite unconsciously she had become a member of a triple
alliance, which kept itself intact in the midst
of the shifting crowd of skaters; but she was
under no temptation to break the tacit bond.
The representative young ladies of Little Rest
were of Miss Esther's age; its young men
were a tradition of the days before the war.
A subsequent and less characteristic crop had
been reaped by the great cities or neighboring factories, by the enticing, devouring frontier, and the equally insatiable sea.

One Saturday evening, after sunset, Charley and Bert had kindled a fire against the
slope of a rock that walled in one side of a
little cove. The shore of the pond, following
the curves of the hill, formed this miniature
bay, where the water, sheltered from wind-
flaws, froze into a sheet of ice, clearer than
that of the open pond. The white, opaque
ice-field beyond was tinted by a rosy reflection from the western sky; above the frozen
stubble-fields the new moon's sickle gleamed.
The skaters were leaving the pond. Cecil was
too far lost in the enchantment of watching
their gypsy fire brighten the edge of twilight,

17

to think of the hour, and the boys were not
likely to remind her.

They had piled stones to make a seat for
her on the windward side of the fire. She sat
with her back against the rock, her muff extended in one hand to shield her face from the
heat. She had a skater's color in her cheeks,
but her lowered lashes gave her eyes a
dreamy look. The wood was already a mass
of brown shadows; around the fire-lit circle
of faces the pale tints of the winter landscape were fading. The blush color in the
west had changed to a cold blue, in which
the new moon gleamed more sharply, but
as yet there were no distinct shadows. The
white ice-shield gathered and diffused the
lingering light.

The boys sat at Cecil's feet, feeding the
flames with snapping cedar-twigs and watching the scattering volleys of sparks. The
smoke-coils floated off and dispersed among
the deepening glooms of the wood.

Cecil was silent, confused by the awakening of a dull heart-ache, the occasional suspen-
sion of which she had called content. She
was restless with the beauty of the evening.

It rankled in her soul. Such evenings were for happy people, or for children, to whom each day was a separate existence. At that moment she would have given all the beauty that enfolded her loneliness, — hushed, dusky wood and glimmering pond, slumberous fields and softly colored twilight, lit by the crescent moon, — for the sky of solid rock, the yellow candle-rays and inky shadows of those rugged underground pastures where she had first recognized the love and the sorrow of her lifetime. With this or with that small circumstance different, how different all might have been! The thought came to her with the agony of an old pain that returns after an interval of rest. She could not recall one moment of absolute happiness that she had ever known through Hilgard, or with him. Their moments together had been clouded by the trouble that was coming to them both; but few and poor as they had been, the memory of them was intolerable now.

What was it, after all, she asked herself, that had separated them? No fatality of their past had kept her from him in his extremity. She would have renewed her broken promise at his death-bed, and felt that it was the sacrament of her life. She could think of him no longer as the dim-eyed figure she had left, prostrate on a sick-bed. But were youth and strength and love of life offences in him for which she held him accountable? Was it not rather her sick faith — her doubt of herself as a positive and vital need to a life already replete? If it were possible to believe that wherever he might be that night he was thinking of her and wanting her! If indeed his happiness were in her gift and he should ask it once more at her hands — what would she do with it? Would she deny him, and bury his hope and hers in her brother's grave, — the old wrongs revenged in the old way, — the hard deeds of men remembered and perpetuated by women!

She rose suddenly to her feet and stood against the rock, receiving upon her full-length figure the strong red glow. The two lads looked up at her, half abashed at her loveliness.

"Come," she said, "let us put out the fire. We must go home! Will you go with me as far as the orchard?" She looked doubtfully

at the lads. She had never before made even
so small a claim as this on their friend-
ship.

Charley grew red with pleasure, but remained silent while Bert answered for both.

"We'll go all the way. But there is a man
coming down through the wood. Let's wait
till he gets by."

The footsteps left the path, and came
crashing and trampling down into the hollow
by the rock. Bert began mentally to take an
attitude of defiance, expecting the usual re-
monstrance from some farmer of the neighborhood, in regard to carelessness with fire.
As the intruder came within the circle of light,
Bert and Charley turned to confront him.
He was tall, youthful, and stalwart of figure,
dressed for a winter journey, in seal-skin cap
and belted ulster. There was a formidable
directness in his glance and bearing. The
boys hesitated a moment, and then fell upon
him with boisterous greetings, and, dragging
him forward, presented him to Cecil as their
brother.

Hilgard had come down to Little Rest in
a despairing pause of his search for Cecil.

He was on the track of the truant lads, but he had not expected to find Cecil with them, encamped like a Romany girl, on the charmed edge of evening, in that remote hollow of the hills. It was an exquisite surprise — a rush of joy, so keen and sweet that it had almost brought the tears to his eyes. She was a radiant figure in the warm fire-glow, but there was no warmth in her greeting.

Cecil knew that he had not come to see her. The bond between them seemed more unreal than ever in the presence of this relationship which she had not even suspected. As she looked at the three who had found each other, she discovered with a fresh pang that she had grown fond of the little lads. She must lose them too, since they belonged with all that she had put out of her life forever. They counted among Hilgard's compensations, — if, indeed, he needed any, — not among hers.   She waited in awkward misery for a chance to escape, while Hilgard submitted to the tumultuous questions of the boys: Where had he kept himself, and why had n't he written?   How long was he going to stay, and would he give them that week in

New York with him at Christmas, as he had promised ?

"Oh, I say! You're not going home without us?" they exclaimed to Cecil, who had turned away toward the wood-path.

"I shall not need you. It will be light enough when I get on the hill."

She did not stop, and her manner was so decided that the lads hesitated, looking puzzled and hurt.

"She asked us to go home with her," they appealed to Hilgard.

"You must first put out that fire, every spark, before you leave it," he said, in the tone of authority that came to his firm voice more readily than tones of tenderness. But the tenderness trembled in it the next moment, when he had followed Cecil, and, walking by her side, his head down close to hers, said, —

"I don't know where home is, but I am going there with you."

"Not to-night. You must leave me to-night."

"I shall never leave you, because I shall never find you again, if I do."

Hilgard's nerve had not quite forsaken him. He felt very quiet, but very desperate. From the shore of the pond came the boys' clear treble shouts as they trod out the sparks and flung the brands of their fire out upon the ice.

"Cecil, let us understand each other now," Hilgard continued. "Did you mean every word in your letter? A woman should not write such a letter as that to a man she does not mean to marry."

"I told you not to come!"

"You may tell that to a sick man. I'm not sick now. I have as good a right to my wife as any man. I have found her, and I mean to make her happy."

Cecil had stopped, moving away from his side in the narrow path.

"It is too much," she said. "No one could bear this!"

"Is my coming too much to bear?"

"Your coming — and your going. It is cruel to keep offering me what I cannot take!"

"You shall take it!" Hilgard put his arms around her and held her fast, with her head

pressed close against his turbulent heart.
" It is not taking, it is giving. Will you give
me nothing for all my love ? Let us end it
here — now. This is the only human way ! "

But Cecil was not yet at rest. In a moment
she drew away from him and listened, with
her hands against his breast, and her cheek
turned toward the faint breeze that blew up
from the hollow.

" Where are the boys ? " she whispered.
The moon hung low over the darkening outline of the hills ; the dim landscape returned
no sound but the rustling of the sear leaves
in the aisles of the wood, and the slight rever-
berations of the ice, warping with the night's
increasing cold.

The lads had not been slow to perceive
that there was a mystery of previous acquaintance between Hilgard and their girl-
comrade, and that their company along the
wood-path was neither missed nor desired.
With hasty, boyish resentment, they had
taken themselves off by another path toward
the village.

" They have gone back alone," Cecil said,
quickly divining her offence against good-

fellowship. " Won't you go after them and bring them back? No, you need n't come back! Stay with them, please, and make them understand!"

Hilgard laughed, a low excited laugh of insecure triumph.

" No, indeed, I won't! The boys will have to wait. They have had their turn."

" But it is not kind, and they *have* a right to you — they have not seen you for so long!"

" I have some rights, myself. They might have seen me if they had told me you were here. Can't you spare *me* a little of your kindness for the boys?"

She put up her cheek close to his bent head.

" I am afraid to begin — if I once *began* to be good to you —"

XVI.

THE PATHS MEET.

HILGARD and Cecil were married on a wet
May morning when the wind that blew across
the farms bore with it the fragrance of rain-
drenched blossoms. In the Hartwell house
a wood-fire lit the gloom of the heavily cur-
tained parlor, where the remnants of the two
families were assembled to witness the marriage ceremony. Mr. Conrath did not lend
his countenance to the proceedings, in any
sense of the word, and it remained for the
grandmother to give away the bride. It was
with a stern reluctance in her heart that she
fulfilled this duty of relationship. The two
women who represented the family of the
bride, wore their dull, black mourning robes,
but Cecil, with pathetic magnanimity, had
put on a gown as white as the happiest omens
might have called for.

In the pauses of the service the soft spring showers dashed in gusts against the window-panes, and rustled in the deep-mouthed chimney. The perfume of hot-house roses stole luxuriously upon the cool, pure air of the old-fashioned room, with a suggestion of the distant city and the men and women of the world outside.

The carriage had not yet come when Cecil entered the parlor in her travelling dress. Mrs. Hartwell was moving about the room with that restlessness upon her which is so much more painful to witness in a large, calm person than in one to whom it is habitual. The boys, on whom every one had counted as a relief to the intensity of the occasion, had developed an unexpected shyness of Hilgard, in his anomalous character of bridegroom. Cecil, very white about the lips and dark about the eyes, sat buttoning her gloves, and trying to listen to the clergyman's voice, prosing gently through the unhappy silence. The fire snapped behind the ponderous brass-work which guarded the grate. Miss Esther sobbed audibly. Hilgard went out into the entry and waited by one of the side-lights, looking down the empty, dripping vista of trees. It was a relief to all, when the spattering of hoofs and the soft roll of wheels sounded on the wet gravel outside, and Hilgard, standing in the doorway, said, " Cecil, the carriage is here."

Mrs. Hartwell crossed the room and folded Cecil, with passionate deliberateness, in her large embrace.

" Oh, say one good word to him before we go!" the girl entreated, in rapid, smothered whispers. " He is my husband. He is your son!"

The grandmother straightened herself. She did not speak, but as she turned away her face and covered it with her handkerchief, she extended one hand to Hilgard with a noble and gracious gesture. He bent above it and kissed it reverently; remembering that it was proffered by one, the latest of whose many sorrows had come through him; whose last pledge of happiness he had made his own.

That evening, Mrs. Hartwell was in her old seat by the fireplace in the back parlor, and Miss Esther was standing at the west window, watching the locust boughs, heavy with their white blossoms, toss in the gale. The rain had ceased, and the struggling moonlight served, as it were, to make visible the wild, soft wind, whose voice they heard in the chimney, and in the creaking of vines against the side of the house.

" Esther, I wish you would set those flowers in the other room. I hate the scent of stale flowers ! " said Mrs. Hartwell.

" But these roses are not faded — just look at them, mother ; I never saw such roses ! "

" They do not please me. There were no such roses when I was a bride. They are too big and too expensive, like everything nowadays. The idea of sending such things to Cecil ! They are about as much like her — "

A vision of Cecil on the empty stool opposite, her elbow resting in one hand, while the other strayed to the pin at her throat, her cheek pressed against the cold marble of the mantel, finished the sentence for the two women. Miss Esther did not look at her mother, who spoke again, breaking the silence with her deep intonation.

" Journeys, journeys, nothing but journeys ! Why could n't they leave her here in peace ? "

" Mother, you know she was not happy here."

" She would have been happy, if he had let her be."

" She would have been happy, perhaps, if she had never seen him," Miss Esther said.

" She never ought to have seen him. It was no place for a young girl. I always said so. There were no such places when I was a girl; the name is enough. There was no such West ! When people went West, they thought about it beforehand ; they consulted their friends ; families went together. They were a long while going, and when they got there, they stayed. There was none of this rushing back and forth, thousands of miles at a stretch ! "

" I don't think it is the journey Cecil minds. And he will take good care of her."

" *He* take care of her ! He is nothing but a boy, himself."

" You cannot deny, mother, that he has a manly look — "

"His looks are well enough. They are nothing but boy and girl, both of them. They might have waited five or ten years; it would have been more fitting, to say the least."

"If they had waited, something else would have happened, very likely. I think it is better to marry young — "

"Than not to marry at all?" Mrs. Hartwell interrupted with scorn. "Why is n't it respectable for a woman, now and then, to stay at home and keep things together for those who go and make a shipwreck of it? Why could n't she have been to you what you have been to me?"

"No, mother. I would not have had that!"

"Have you found it so hard?"

"Mother, you should be the last to ask that! You know it is all the life I could have had. But it would have crushed Cecil, after what was past. And it would n't have been fair to him."

"He seems to have been quite able to look out for himself." She had sunk, from the effort by which, at the last, she had accepted Hilgard, into a querulous bitterness towards him that would last while the reaction lasted.

" Those were nice boys — his brothers," she added, more gently.

" Half-brothers," Miss Esther corrected.

" One of them is very like him in looks," her mother continued. " Did you say they were staying here ? What can they be doing here ? "

" They are pupils of Mr. Lyle's."

" Well, that is n't a bad place for them. When you send out the cake, Esther, I wish you would send them plenty — what boys call plenty. Perhaps Mr. Lyle will let them come up to tea, some Sunday night."

" He might like to come with them," Miss Esther suggested, meekly.

" I dare say he would, but I don't think I care about him. He is well enough, but the boys will have a better time without him."

Miss Esther carried the roses into the front parlor, where she remained a few moments, setting chairs back into their places, and closing shutters for the night. She paused before the open piano, and laid her hand on the cold, soundless key-board. The worn ivory sank under her touch, breaking the stillness of the room with its helpless discord. She closed the piano with a dull clap of the lid, and leaned upon it while the murmurs of the imprisoned chords within prolonged the sound. To her wistful ear the room was haunted by echoes of dumb music, — songs that had been sung there; quick, unsteady sallies of childish feet; laughter of young girls; whispered vows that death had broken; stifled sobs and prayers for the dead.

"Esther, I want you," her mother called, from the inner room. "Come close to me, child. We have got the house all to ourselves again. Do you think I am a hard old woman? Oh, I miss my children! I miss them every day and every night." She reached out blindly and gathered her daughter into her arms. "I had set my foolish old heart upon the child. She was the last one. She filled the empty place. She suited me."

"She suited him, too," Miss Esther said, in a broken voice. "She suited us all! Even her father was proud of her — though he said she had no manner, and never would have!"

"Manner!" the old lady repeated, wrathfully. "She had heart!" They spoke of Cecil as if she were already with the past, in which their thoughts habitually dwelt.

XVII.

EXIT SHOSHONE.

THE successor of Hilgard and Conrath in the management of the Consolidated Led-Horse and Shoshone mines was one day searching out the corner monuments of the original claims.

The young pines in the gulch — which, instead of dividing, now united the two properties — had counted another circle of concentric growth. The aspens again bore their frail golden fleece, a prize for the rapacious autumn winds. The Shoshone dwelling-house had been converted into a miners' boarding-house, presided over by Molly, the wife of the ex-timberman, now night foreman on the Led-Horse division, and the path where Cecil had taken her solitary walks was graded into a road for ore-wagons.

The history of the Led-Horse and the Shoshone was the history of the camp, epitomized. The stormy beginning of days was over; the illegitimate forces were under control, and such a rude challenge as that which had tested Hilgard's leadership had not been known in the camp since his effectual and impressive acceptance of the issue. The public value of his deed it was not given him to know. He had only known its sharp recoil upon himself.

The superintendent was studying the inscriptions on the low monument stones in the bottom of the gulch. A slight golden glitter led his eyes to the spot where a ring lay, half embedded in the brown pine-needles, which had borne the weight of the winter's snows.

He rubbed away the earth clinging to the words heavily embossed on its outer circle: *Dieu vous garde.* In the inner circle he read the faint lettering: *C. C. from H. C.* He slipped the ring on his smallest finger; it would not pass the middle joint.

The superintendent had heard of Conrath's sister, the fair young girl who had presided over the Shoshone household during its stormiest epoch, and had vaguely wondered what part, if any, might have been hers in its

CECIL'S RING.

history. He was not so mature as to have
lost sight of the fateful nature of the feminine element, even in mining complications,
but he had not found it easy to believe in the
existence of a young girl, such as Miss Conrath had been described, in such a place,
under such circumstances. It had been his
experience that women generally fitted the
places where they were found, and the men
who were their companions. Here, however,
was presumptive proof of civilized feminine
occupation at an early period of the Shoshone
history. He carried the ring a week or more,
each day intending to express it eastward,
and finally sent it, directed to the office of
the Consolidated Company, to be forwarded
to Miss Conrath. It was not without a faint
sentiment of regret that he parted with the
one gentle association connected with the
story of the Shoshone tragedy.

He leaned against the counter of the express office, waiting for his receipt, and watching, meanwhile, the weighing of one of those
long pine boxes which form part of the freight
of every overland train.

"Who is that they 're shipping East?" one

of the loungers at the counter inquired of
the express agent.

"Don't you remember — young fellow got
shot, up at the Shoshone, a year ago?"

"Oh, yes — jumpin' scrape, was n't it?"

"Yes. He just about closed out the jumpin'
business in this camp."

"I thought they planted him for good,"
another voice struck in. "They made row
enough about it!"

"Oh, that was Gashwiler's racket. Pity
they had n't planted him instead!"

"What's *come* of old Gash?" the first
speaker asked, of the company, generally.

"Last *I* heard of him he was stealin'
Indian ponies over on the reservation."

"Two ninety-seven," the man at the scale
called to the clerk. He printed the number
of pounds weight upon the lid of the box,
and swept, with one stroke of his marking-
brush, a black circle around the figures.

Conrath was going home at last. The
camp lightly remembered his misdeeds; but
the women who had waited long for his body
to be brought to them from the alien soil where
it had lain, kept a different record — a record

in which all was forgotten save the good they had known of him.

They made his grave beside an older one, the headstone of which bore the name of Cecilia Hartwell, wife of Robert Conrath, who had died in the twenty-eighth year of her life and the sixth year of her marriage. The matted growth of periwinkle which had woven its coverlet of dark and shining leaves above the mother's bed, before another winter's snows had whitened it and another summer had starred it with purple blossoms had crept half across the new-made grave. One might fancy the mother, in her sleep, reaching out unconsciously and covering her child.

A...............................tion

*A series of repri...........9th century American novels important
to the study of American folklore, culture and literary history*

THOMAS BAILEY ALDRICH
The Stillwater Tragedy

JAMES LANE ALLEN
A Kentucky Cardinal

GERTRUDE ATHERTON
Los Cerritos: A Romance of Modern Times
The Californians
Senator North
Aristocrats
The Splendid Idle Forties

ARLO BATES
The Puritans

OLIVER THOMAS BEARD
Bristling With Thorns

ALICE BROWN
Tiverton Tales
The County Road

FRANCIS H. BURNETT
Through One Administration

WILLIAM A. CARUTHERS
Kentuckian in New York, or the Adventures of Three Southerns
The Cavaliers of Virginia

CHARLES WADDELL CHESNUTT
The Conjure Woman
The Wife of His Youth; and Other Stories of the Colour Line
The House Behind the Cedars

KATE CHOPIN
Bayou Folk

JOHN ESTEN COOKE
The Virginia Comedians
Surry of Eagle's Nest
Mohun: or the Last Days of Lee and His Paladins
My Lady Pokahontas

ROSE TERRY COOKE
Rootbound and Other Sketches

MARGARET DELAND
John Ward, Preacher

THOMAS DIXON
The Leopard's Spots
The Clansman

EDWARD EGGLESTON
Roxy
The Faith Doctor

MARY HALLOCK FOOTE
The Led-Horse Claim

PAUL LEICESTER FORD
The Honorable Peter Stirling

HAROLD FREDERIC
Seth's Brother's Wife

MARY E. WILKINS FREEMAN
A New England Nun; and Other Stories
The Portion of Labor

HENRY B. FULLER
The Cliff Dwellers